P9-CQV-806

MOONFLETE

BOOKS-BY-MAIL
3301 JEFFERSON AVENUE S.W.
BIRMINGHAM, AL 35221
(205) 925-6178

MOONFLETE

Veronica Black

This Large Print edition is published by BBC Audiobooks Ltd, Bath, England and by Thorndike Press®, Waterville, Maine, USA.

Published in 2004 in the U.K. by arrangement with Robert Hale Limited.

Published in 2004 in the U.S. by arrangement with Robert Hale, Ltd.

U.K. Hardcover ISBN 0–7540–6958–3 (Chivers Large Print)
U.K. Softcover   ISBN 0–7540–6959–1 (Camden Large Print)
U.S. Softcover   ISBN 0–7862–6603–1 (Nightingale)

Copyright © Veronica Black 1972

All rights reserved.

The text of this Large Print edition is unabridged.
Other aspects of the book may vary from the original edition.

Set in 16 pt. New Times Roman.

Printed in Great Britain on acid-free paper.

British Library Cataloguing in Publication Data available

Library of Congress Control Number: 2004103119

CHAPTER ONE

It is strange now to remember that I never even heard of 'Moonflete' until I was eighteen years old. I lived without knowing that such a place existed or that the Fletchers—the other Fletchers—lived there. Now it seems to me that there never was a time when the house, and the courtyard, and the view across the valley was not the centre of my world. There never was a time when I was not familiar with the tapping of Heather's stick along the gallery, and Cherry's laughter ringing out by the pool. Yet, until I was eighteen, I knew nothing of these.

I grew up in London in a tall, narrow house in a long, narrow street. The house had plush velvet curtains at the window with lace nets stretched behind them tightly across the glass, so that one saw the street through a mesh of tiny holes and spidery thread. There was a sooty little garden at the back with speckled laurel bushes and a vegetable patch that was choked with weeds for most of the time, as none of us were very keen gardeners. By 'us' I mean Miss Trimlett, Perkins, Cook, Lavinia the parlour maid, and me.

My name is Melody, and my surname was Fletcher. Miss Trimlett was my governess. She had been with me for as long as I could remember. Indeed I took her completely for granted, just as I took for granted the fact that we never went anywhere to see anybody and that nobody ever came to see us. If I ever thought about it all, I assumed that we had no friends because I was so unusual-looking that nobody wanted to know me.

I was about seven, I think, and had been taken to the pantomime for my birthday treat. It was then I discovered why I looked so different from everybody else. Up to that time I had disliked my face without trying to discover *why* my eyes slanted up at the corners and my skin was yellowish. But as I came out of the theatre, with Miss Trimlett holding my hand, and Perkins hurrying to wave down a cab, a group of children just behind us swarmed out.

'Oh, do look, Bella!' one of them said. 'It's a Chink.'

The older children in the group hushed him but he went on pointing at me.

'But it is! I saw lots of them in my picture book!'

Miss Trimlett gripped my hand tightly and fairly hustled me into the cab, where she sat with her hands and lips folded angrily together all the way home. But when we did get home, she let me have an extra slice of chocolate cake for tea. While I was eating it, she looked at me several times as if she wanted to say something but wasn't certain how to begin.

2

'It's very ill-bred to make remarks about people!' she exclaimed crossly.

'What is a Chink?' I enquired. 'The little boy said I was one. What is it?'

'It's a person with Chinese blood,' she told me, 'but the term is slang and is not used by polite people.'

'But I don't come from China,' I pointed out logically.

'No, my dear, but I understand that your mother did,' she said.

'Is she dead?'

'As far as I know, dear. I'm afraid I know very little of your family.'

I was not, at that age, very much interested. It was, I suppose, a tribute to my governess's rearing of me that I felt too secure to bother much about relatives I had never seen. It was not until much later, when I was about fourteen, that I began to ask about my father. Miss Trimlett, however, could tell me very little.

'I believe he is alive, but as to his whereabouts, or how he makes his living I cannot tell you, for I never met him.'

'Never met him? Then how did I get here?' Filled with ideas picked up from the novels I smuggled in from the Circulating Library, I asked hopefully, 'Did you find me on the doorstep?'

'Good gracious, no! What an idea!' My governess looked quite shocked. 'I was

3

engaged when you were three years old. An advertisement in the newspaper attracted my attention. My former pupil had just come out in society and I was looking for a new post.'

'And you came to look after me?'

'I answered the advertisement and received a letter asking me to present myself at Brown's Hotel for an interview,' she answered in her precise unhurried way. 'The gentleman who interviewed me was quite elderly, but obviously cultured. He gave his name as Briggs and, without actually saying so, conveyed the impression that he was in the legal profession. He informed me that a competent person was needed to take charge of a three-year-old girl, of part Chinese origin. The woman who had been taking care of you had died during the influenza epidemic, and a replacement was needed at once.'

'But didn't he tell you anything else?'

'He gave me your name and mentioned that your mother had been a Chinese lady. He conveyed the impression, again without stating it explicitly, that your father was alive. I came here and remained here.'

'But how do we get the money to pay the servants?' I asked.

'I receive a large bank-draft every month out of which I pay all personal and household expenses,' she told me. 'Perkins and Cook and Lavinia were all engaged in the same way when you were a baby.'

4

'And the woman who looked after me before you came?'

'A Mrs. Ackers, a very quiet, respectable lady, so the others told me.'

'But if anything happened to me, how would you let anybody know?'

'I have instructions to leave any urgent message at the bank. Fortunately, there has never been any necessity to do so. You are small for your age, but you have always been remarkably healthy.'

And slant-eyed and yellow skinned, I thought. If I do have any relatives it's no wonder they don't want me!

Afterwards, I speculated occasionally about my parents. If they were dead, then who paid the bank-draft every month? It was signed, said Miss Trimlett, by Mr. Briggs, but she had not laid eyes on him in person since that first interview in Brown's Hotel. I decided that if I had been my governess, I would have gone more deeply into the matter but when I had the bright idea of going to Somerset House to look for my birth certificate, she looked aghast at the suggestion.

'My dear, that would be a very vulgar and ill-bred course to take. Indeed I am a little shocked that a pupil of mine should contemplate such action. Depend upon it that your father, or whoever made these arrangements, must have had an excellent reason for so doing, and it is not for us to question.'

I thought rather differently on the subject but I kept my thoughts to myself. It was never a habit of mine to rebel openly, but one day I promised myself that I would go quietly along and obtain the information for myself. For the present I had too much respect and affection for Miss Trimlett to defy her wishes.

So we went on living in the tall, narrow house where nothing ever changed. I used to sit by my bedroom window at night sometimes and watch the gas-lit street through the lace curtains. Often a couple would stroll past, entwined together in the pools of radiance between the shadows and I would wonder what it must be like to have a male escort in the tranquil evenings. Not that I was ever likely to find out. At that period the ideal woman was tall and full-busted with wide hips and a swanlike neck. I was small and thin with the added disadvantages of Chinese eyes and skin, and straight, heavy black hair that utterly refused to curl or to frizz into a pompadour. No gentleman would ever desire to stroll with me through lamplit streets and I saw myself, growing older, still living with Miss Trimlett. Though I no longer had regular instruction from her, we read a portion of French and a portion of English literature together every day, and she gave me daily sketching and music lessons. It was a placid routine, but not one that I looked forward to following for the rest of my life.

Perhaps that was why I so often took refuge in fantastic daydreams. One day, I thought, a tall, handsome man will drive up in a fine carriage with a crest on the door. He will lean out of the window and smile at me.

'My dear Melody!' he will say. 'You cannot imagine how fervently I have longed to greet my daughter!'

Stuff and nonsense, of course! If my father still lived there was no reason in the world why he shouldn't either visit me or send for me. Obviously, he didn't want me, and who *would* want me? I was ugly and half-foreign with no particular charm or talents. Even the fashions of the time were against me. I was swamped by shawl and crinoline skirt and deep brimmed bonnet. The stylish shades of magenta and lilac made me look as if I were in the last stages of some dreadful disease of the liver. Perhaps I ought to hire myself out to an organ-grinder, I thought, and was glad that I had at least retained a sense of humour. Had anybody told me that my whole life was about to change suddenly and so dramatically that the world would never be the same again, I would have laughed aloud.

In the January of eighteen sixty-two I was eighteen years old. I always took particular interest in my birthday. My name and my date of birth, given to Miss Trimlett by Mr. Biggs, were all the facts about myself that I

7

possessed.

On that morning I went out into the garden as usual to fill the bird tray with scraps of bread and twists of bacon-rind. It was bitterly cold with snow thick on the ground and a freezing wind howling up the covered entry that separated our house from the next. There were footprints across the snow, leading from the entry to the bird tray. For a moment I thought that Perkins must have tramped out earlier with some food but the prints were small and shallow. Perkins had broad, flat feet.

There was something on the bird tray. I reached up and took down a small, flat parcel covered with snow. The inscription 'Melody Fletcher' in thick, black ink had smeared a little in the dampness. I held the parcel in one hand, scattering bread and bacon from the other with scant regard as to where they fell. It had just begun to snow again and the footprints were already being obliterated.

I hurried indoors and found Miss Trimlett at the breakfast table. By my plate was a neatly wrapped parcel. It would contain books or a flat bottle of Eau-de-Cologne. My governess invariably gave me one or the other.

'Miss Trimlett, did you see anybody go into the garden and put this on the bird tray? I just found it there.' I held up the damp little package.

'No, indeed I didn't. What a very eccentric thing to do! But who would put something

8

there?' she asked in surprise.

'That's what I'm going to discover. Who knows it's my birthday today?'

As I spoke I wrenched off the wrappings to reveal a wooden box, very shallow and square and highly polished. I stared at it feeling a sudden, irrational reluctance to lift the lid.

'Do open it.' Miss Trimlett's mild curiosity—she was the least inquisitive of women—had been aroused.

I lifted the lid slowly and looked down at a silver chain, coiled round and set with milky, bluish-white stones.

'A necklace,' I said blankly and lifted it out. 'It's rather beautiful, isn't it?'

The chain was finely wrought, the stones evenly ranged along its length, twelve small ones and in the centre of a larger one, each milky disc set in the delicate silver.

'And valuable too.' Miss Trimlett rose from her place and came to my side. 'Those are moonstones. My dear mother once had a little moonstone brooch which I used to think was very pretty. These are beautifully matched.'

'Thirteen of them,' I said and a little chill ran up my spine.

'You really cannot accept such an expensive present,' Miss Trimlett worried.

'I can't give it back either,' I pointed out.

'I cannot imagine who could have left it for you,' she continued. 'If anybody wanted to buy you a gift, why did they leave it in the bird tray? Why not leave it on the step?'

'In this weather it might have been snowed over and accidentally kicked aside,' I suggested. 'I go out every day to feed the birds.'

I stopped, realising that the garden was at the back of the house. Beyond was a low wall dividing us from the lane that ran along the row of houses. People frequently used the lane as a short cut and many of them must have seen me putting out the bread and bacon-rind.

'You will hardly wear it,' Miss Trimlett frowned.

Up to that moment I had had no intention of wearing it. Despite its beauty, the thirteen stones combined with the mysterious manner of its arrival invested it with a sinister quality. But Miss Trimlett's bland assertion irritated me.

'Of course I'll wear it,' I said and fastened it carefully about my throat, where it shimmered in the looking-glass, above the collar of my grey dress. It looked wrong somehow. A low-necked ballgown would have set it off more suitably.

'I bought you a small gift too,' my governess hinted.

I felt a pang of guilt. Poor Miss Trimlett had nobody for whom to buy presents except me, and I had wasted time on a gift of unknown origin. I went swiftly to the table, opening the book, a copy of Wordsworth's *Poems* and exclaiming in what I hope was well-simulated surprise and pleasure. But the silver chain was cool about my neck and the milky stones had a pale, hypnotic gleam, drawing my eyes frequently to the mirror. Later I tucked the necklace beneath the collar of my dress and felt its light pressure against my skin.

I could not help thinking about the women who must have worn the necklace in the past. That it was old was evident, for the clasp was very slightly marked, and the setting of the stones was not modern.

But more than external appearance proved it had belonged to others before me. The milky stones held something in their depths that made me shiver a little, though I could not tell why. It was almost as if they held some memory that was not part of my own experience; a memory that clung to them as subtly and searchingly as perfume from the pressed leaves of a dead rose.

Miss Trimlett would have considered my fancies as indicative of an unsettled stomach and a weakness of purpose, so I said nothing but often, when we sat reading or sewing, my fingers would stray to the high collar of my dress and I would feel the cool discs against my flesh, and know against all reason that the necklace was destined to be very important for me.

It was in March that the letter came. As I had never in my life received a letter before,

11

its effect on me was quite disproportionate to its appearance. There was absolutely nothing in a letter to make one shiver with a mixture of excitement and apprehension. Yet I stood for several minutes, before I broke the wafer, and read the closely written, carefully folded paper within. It was headed:

Moonflete,
Jason,
Lancs.

Moonflete. A strange name, I thought, full of romantic echoes. The letter was undated and there was no opening salutation though it had been addressed to me.

I require my daughter to visit me at the above address on Saturday, the fifteenth of March, eighteen sixty-two. She will travel alone without luggage to Manchester arriving at noon and will wait there for Yang. He will give her further instructions. She will not write to me or communicate with me in any way before that date.
Sincerely,
Eben Fletcher.

So that was my father's name. Eben Fletcher of Moonflete, in Jason. My father, writing in the third person as coldly as if I were some business acquaintance.

I handed it to Miss Trimlett.

'He does say only a visit, my dear,' she observed, having read it through. 'It doesn't sound as if he requires me to make other arrangements.'

Poor Miss Trimlett! At that moment all that concerned her was the fear she might be forced to seek another post.

'I wouldn't dream of staying with him permanently,' I said, indignantly. 'You have brought me up and he's never taken any notice of my existence. Yet he snaps his fingers and expects me to come running! The tone of that letter!'

'I imagine it was enclosed in another letter,' Miss Trimlett said, studying the missive more closely. 'Depend upon it, my dear, but this was forwarded. By the bank, I think, for it was certainly posted in London.'

'Dear Sir, Kindly forward the enclosed to my daughter whom I have a fancy to examine,' I said crossly. 'And after eighteen years I must jump on the first train going north, to please a father I never knew!'

'I could enquire at the bank,' she suggested. 'They would tell me if they had posted on a letter. But it seems odd that he didn't write directly to you.'

'He evidently doesn't think of me as a person at all, simply as a piece of property about to be transferred.' I hesitated and then burst out. 'I've a very good mind not to go at

13

all! Let him come to London if he wants to see me.'

But I knew that wild horses wouldn't be able to drag me from the Manchester train. The summons had awoken in me not only resentment but the most intense curiosity.

The next day, Miss Trimlett came back from her visit to the bank to inform me that her surmise had been correct. The letter had been enclosed in another, asking for it to be posted on.

'I did venture to ask if Mr. Fletcher wrote to them often,' she confessed, 'but they are so very discreet—as, of course, they have to be, my dear, that I'm afraid I got no satisfactory reply.'

And so I was bound for a place called Moonflete, I thought. Jason must be a very tiny village for it wasn't marked on any map we could find. It must be within easy travelling distance of Manchester. In any event, Yang would meet me. Who in the world was Yang? The name had an Oriental ring.

Miss Trimlett was obviously deeply concerned. She thought of me still as a child, and children were not packed into trains and despatched to unknown places. Neither, for that matter, were well-bred young ladies.

'*And* without any luggage!' she mourned, as if that were the ultimate in depravity.

'I don't believe that I stand in the least danger,' I told her frankly.

14

No gentleman would look at me twice, except out of curiosity. But the cool stones round my neck seemed to remind me that there might be other dangers beyond the peril of being accosted when travelling alone.

CHAPTER TWO

1862

At noon on the fifteenth of March, I stepped out of the train at Manchester after a journey which, despite all Miss Trimlett's fears, had proved completely uneventful. As I had expected, only one or two people have given me a cursory glance. I was dressed inconspicuously in a grey travelling dress and mantle, with a bonnet that shadowed my face. Cook, bursting with unasked questions, had packed sandwiches and apple-pie in a small, covered basket, and I ate them as I sat in my corner-seat, watching the towns and patches of countryside slide past. The moonstone necklace lay around my neck under my bodice, and in my reticule was the summons sent on by the bank. I tried to remain calm and cool, but mingled with the very natural excitement at my first rail journey was the curiosity that bubbled up in me whenever I thought of seeing my father for the first time.

The station was large, grimy and noisy, packed with people hurrying up and down. I stood uncertainly, watching relatives and friends greeting one another. It gave me an odd, lonely sensation to stand in the midst of a crowd and not know where to go or what to do next. I drew away and stood at the fringe of the various groups, wondering how I would be seen by the person called Yang, or how he would recognise me.

Then, through a gap, I saw a small yellow-skinned man making his way towards me. He wore a dark blue coat that flapped about his ankles and under the flat blue cap on his head stuck out a short, greasy pigtail. He was shuffling, peering intently into the faces of those he passed. At that moment I could have turned, melted away into the crowd, and got on the next train back to London. Something inside me screamed out to do just that, but the moment passed and the little Chinaman leaned forward, peered under the brim of my bonnet, and softly lisped.

'Missy Melody? Missy Melody?'

I nodded and the old man put the tips of his hands together and bowed.

'You are so very much like Madam Silver Moon,' he said, and his slit eyes filled with tears. I was half-afraid that I was about to be embraced but he bowed again.

'I am Yang, body-servant to Madam and now body-servant to Missy. Will you please come with me now?'

I nodded again, and then, lest he think me

16

dumb or half-witted, said, 'Is it very far to Jason?'

'Three hours, four hours, five hours if the rain begins. We drive there in the coach.'

So, after all there would be a coach. But when I gave in my ticket and passed through the barrier, Yang led the way across the cobbled road to a small and shabby conveyance with two sturdy horses waiting between the shafts.

'This is not fitting for Missy,' Yang said, opening the door. 'But it was Master's wish that I bring you quiet, very quiet, to Moonflete. You will please excuse?'

The interior was clean and comfortable. I accepted Yang's dry yellow claw and climbed up the step into the vehicle. The door closed and a minute or two later we rolled through narrow streets past buildings grimed with soot.

It looked a dismal, dreary place and many of the people in the streets were thin and ragged. I had seen poor people in the south too but they had a brash, Cockney gaiety. The people who glanced apathetically at our vehicle as it passed them wore their rags with a proud, stubborn, despairing air.

I was glad when we left the town and began to travel slowly through fields and smaller villages. Though still soot-grimed, the houses were pretty with pots of flowers in the windows and washing strung out jauntily on the lines. The sun was shining, and above the rattling of

17

the wheels I could hear the wind moaning as we climbed high, and then dipped down into little valleys, fed by streams that wandered between tussocks of grass on which lean grey sheep, many with young lambs, patiently grazed.

After a while, lulled by the rocking of the carriage, I dozed a little. The light was changing, the gloom of a northern spring casting a pall over the landscape. When I woke up, the colour had drained out of grass and sky and the howling of the wind was more intense, shrieking through the rattling windows of the coach.

We were dipping down again into a steep valley and opposite, by dint of craning my neck, I could see a road winding uphill between sloping moorland, with the darker roofs of houses dotted here and there.

I sat up, straightening my bonnet and pulling my mantle more trimly round my shoulders. I sensed that we were drawing near our destination and a tremor of something very like fear ran through me. It was stupid to feel afraid when I was only going to meet my father. But the landscape appeared so desolate and the sunshine had vanished.

We stopped abruptly and a moment later, Yang opened the door and put out his hand to help me alight. As I descended I looked about a cobbled yard with stables on every side. There were one or two empty stalls; in the others horses chewed placidly, their soft eyes indifferent.

'If Missy will come with me now?' Yang said.

'Yes, of course.'

My tone was doubtful, for the complete absence of any other person, the arrival in the stableyard instead of before the front door, the whispering servility of the old Chinaman—all combined to produce in me a feeling of quivering apprehension.

'This way, Missy.'

Yang bowed and led me along a narrow entry, up a flight of stone steps, and into a house whose outlines glimmered faintly through the dusk. We were evidently in the back regions. I could hear the clatter of dishes and we passed a pantry crowded with shelves of preserves and marmalades. Yang went ahead of me up a flight of stairs carpeted with heavy floral patterned broadloom. The bannister under my hand flowed up in a smooth curve of gleaming dark wood. Coloured lozenges of light dyed his shabby blue coat. I looked up and saw a stained glass window at the head of the stairs and a wide passage stretching to left and right of that.

Yang turned to the left and I followed him past a series of closed doors to a door at the end. Before this, Yang bowed again and then motioned me to follow him within. I hesitated and then stepped through.

19

I had read fairy tales where the heroine was transported to some magical land where the sun always shone and the flowers always grew. For an instant it seemed as if I had become such a heroine and I stood quite still, looking round in delight.

It was a bedroom, white walled and white carpeted. Instinctively I glanced at my feet and was glad I had remembered to wipe my shoes as I came in. White velvet curtains hung at the three long windows and the great four-poster bed was hung with the same material. The few pieces of furniture in the room were painted white—the sofa and the two armchairs piled with white cushions. One wall was occupied by a series of fitted cupboards and wardrobes and in another corner was a cabinet painted white and decorated with silver dragons. The only notes of colour in the room were two vases of a deep, dark blue which stood on the mantelshelf above a ready-laid but unlit fire. They flanked an ivory clock and on the wall above was spread an enormous fan of peacock feathers.

'This was Madame Silver Moon's room,' Yang said. 'Now it is Missy Melody's room.'

'It's very beautiful. You've prepared it so well.'

I wanted to be pleasant but the old man's intent, adoring gaze made me feel uncomfortable.

'Missy will please put on these clothes?' He

20

opened one of the cupboard doors where some garments were hanging and then indicated another door, saying, 'That is the dressing-room. When Missy is ready, I will return.'

'And when will I see my father?' I enquired.

To my surprise, Yang shook his head.

'I will return when Missy is dressed,' he said again and bowed, palms together, before he shuffled out.

I went over to the window and looked out but could discern nothing except darkening grass sweeping to a red-tinged horizon. There were oil lamps already lit on a table by the bed and on the dragon-painted cabinet, and their soft light seemed to intensify the cool purity of my surroundings. The clothes in the wardrobe were unlike any I had seen before. I took out the ones to which Yang had pointed and spread them on the bed. There was a pair of slim trousers in honey-coloured silk, a high collared, long sleeved tunic of the same shade, embroidered thickly with tiny orange and gold butterflies; flat heeled tiny leather slippers, a gold fan. The slippers were unworn but there was a snag in the embroidered tunic.

Obviously these things had belonged to Silver Moon—to my mother. I longed suddenly to dress up in them, to see what I looked like in Chinese costume.

The inner door opened into another room, smaller than the bedroom but still white. A sunken bath, an enormous dressing-table filled with brushes and combs and innumerable bottles met my astonished gaze. There was no window in this room, but mirrors lined the walls and ceiling so that everywhere I turned I saw myself reflected. There was another door near the dressing-table but when I turned the handle it remained closed. The dressing-table itself held two lighted lamps. I sat down on the stool before it and began to open some of the bottles and jars. A subtle medley of perfumes rose to my nostrils—rose, jasmine, musk, sandalwood.

I imagined how Silver Moon must have sat here before me, dipping her fingers into the perfumed oils, seeing herself reflected in the mirrors. One thing was clear. Whatever feelings my father entertained for me, he had adored my mother. These were the apartments and belongings of a deeply-loved woman.

Behind me, a voice said softly, 'Missy? Oh, Missy!'

I swung round, and looked into a small yellow face with grey hair braided tightly round her head. I had not heard anybody approach and I suppose my startled look showed.

'Forgive me, please,' the old woman said, quickly. 'It is not my place to enter without warning. I am Astra, body-servant to Madam Silver Moon, and now body-servant to Missy Melody.'

'It was you who lit the lamps!'

'Yes, Missy. I am here now to help you to dress.'

I saw that she had the honey-coloured outfit draped carefully over her arm. She herself wore a wide pair of faded blue trousers under a shapeless tunic, and there were tiny golden hoops in her pierced ears. Her face was old and gentle, and her voice had a hypnotic, sing-song quality. I steeled myself against it and spoke briskly, in my best imitation of Miss Trimlett.

'And then I can meet my father.'

'As to that, it is for Yang to say,' she answered tranquilly.

I had different ideas, but I said nothing and allowed her to help me off with my bonnet and mantle. She moved quietly and quickly, her deft fingers unhooking my bodice. As my dress slipped from my shoulders, the fingers ceased to move and turning, puzzled, to glance at her I saw her eyes riveted to the moonstone necklace.

'What is it? What's the matter?' I asked sharply.

Her yellow skin was an unpleasant, sickly grey and I had never seen such terror on a human face before.

'What is it?' I asked once more.

But the expression on her face was tranquil again.

'I grow old and forgetful,' she said, dragging

her eyes from the necklace. 'You must be patient, Missy, with a stupid old woman.'

There was no point at that moment in questioning her further. She was lifting the crinoline frame over my head, holding out the silk trousers. I stepped into them and allowed her to hook up the tunic at the back.

'The garments fit Missy very well,' she observed with complacency. 'The Master hoped very much it would be so. The sandals he bought in many sizes, for he feared that your feet would be enormous.'

She sighed deeply and looked down at my narrow feet as if the Master's worst fears had been realised.

'Now I will comb Missy's hair and you shall see,' Astra went on. 'Madam Silver Moon could sit upon her tresses.'

My own black hair was waist-length. It was soothing to have it combed, drawn to one side and plaited. Some of the tension went out of my back and neck as she worked, humming under her breath as she did so. I closed my eyes, relaxing as she began to smooth lotion into my hands and face. The lotion smelled of jasmine.

'Now Missy will please to look,' Astra ordered softly.

I opened my eyes and saw myself reflected in the mirrors. It was hard to believe these were all images of me. I was sallow and plain and unusual-looking, but the girls in the mirrors were tiny and exotic with eyes slanting in an impish, golden face and blue-black hair drawn over one shoulder in a thick plait.

'If a jewel has not the right setting, it will not glow,' said Astra. 'You are so like Madam. So like!'

'You were fond of my mother, weren't you?' I said.

'I worshipped her,' Astra said simply. 'Yang and I worshipped her.'

'You were with her a long time, I suppose?'

'When she was a baby. We came with her on the ship from the Forbidden City. Twenty years ago. At that time I could speak no English. But now I will call Yang and tell him you are all prepared.'

She gave the customary little bow and glided swiftly away. I allowed myself the indulgence of a further glance in the mirrors and went through again into the big, white bedroom. Yang was waiting respectfully by the door. When he saw me his face lit up and I knew he was remembering my mother.

'I'd like to go and see my father now,' I told him.

'It would be better for Missy to have her supper first. Master is not ready,' he began, but I interrupted briskly.

'Then Master will have to bestir himself, won't he? After eighteen years I expect to meet my father as soon as possible after my arrival. Where is he?'

'Master is in the library,' Yang said reluctantly.

'Then we'll go to the library. Please take me there at once.'

I was not used to giving orders but the old man was obviously used to receiving them, for after the briefest hesitation, he bowed and led the way back along the corridor and down the wide staircase where we turned into another passage, lit at intervals by lamps set in niches along the white panelled walls. Halfway down the servant paused before a double-door and stood aside politely.

Now that the moment was upon me, I felt quite calm and confident. Perhaps it was the self-assurance that comes from knowing that one is wearing lovely clothes and looking one's best, perhaps it was the freedom of tunic and trousers after constricting whalebone, but I suddenly felt as if I were capable of dealing with whatever lay in store for me.

I tapped on the door and went in without waiting for an invitation. The room was brightly lighted—so bright that I was momentarily dazzled. The light came from oil lamps—there must have been at least thirty of them, ranged on every available surface. Three even stood in the hearth before the empty grate. The apartment, despite the lamps, was cold and stuffy. It struck chill through the thin silk of my tunic.

I gazed round at the high-backed leather

26

chairs, the filled bookshelves towering to the ceiling, the curtained alcove from which more light was streaming. There was a movement behind the curtains and a feeling of intense irritation swept over me. This nonsense, I considered, had gone quite far enough. Up to now, my father seemed to have been putting me through a series of tests, manipulating me as if I were a puppet. And I was becoming heartily sick of being manipulated.

Crossly I strode forward and pulled aside the curtains stifling a shriek as a small black cat leapt past me, miaowing frantically. Then my eyes moved to the table within the alcove. I had never seen a coffin before but I knew it at once and knew too the name of the old man who lay within. An old, white-haired man with closed eyes and a beak of a nose pointing up to the ceiling.

I stared at the open coffin and felt a scream bubble up in my throat and die before it reached my lips. Then I backed away very slowly, through the parted curtains and across the brilliantly lit apartment. I was afraid to take my eyes from that still figure in the open coffin. My hand caught at the door-knob, twisted it, pulled the door towards me. And I was in the passage again, with the slit-eyed Yang still watching me from the shadows.

I turned and ran in the opposite direction, along the corridor to the door at the far end. My fingers scrabbled on the panels for a moment, turned the carved knob, and I stood, outlined in lamplight, looking down a flight of six or seven steps into a room heavy with the perfume of flowers.

There was a group of people within the room, lounging at their ease in cushioned chairs, save for one elderly lady in black who sat in an upright chair, knitting sedately. They had all heard the opening of the door and looked up, arrested in movement and conversation. Then the elderly lady dropped her knitting and put up her hands as if to ward me off.

'Silver Moon!' she screamed. 'Oh, my God! It's Silver Moon!'

CHAPTER THREE

That was the moment when I saw them all for the first time, and would never see any of them so clearly again, because I looked at them without preconceived ideas and my shocked mind retained a picture of them as they stared at me, so that in the time which followed I often conjured it up in an effort to make sense of everything.

The elderly woman in the black dress who had screamed and dropped her knitting, now sat with raised hands, staring at me with fear and repulsion in her lined face. The other woman in the group, blonde ringlets gleaming against a black evening gown, sat with her mouth open in a rosy, childlike face. The other three members of the circle were male. The oldest of the three was a portly man, clutching a glass of something like brandy in a heavily ringed hand as if he were a drowning man hanging on to a rope. The second man was in shadow, only his long legs in high riding boots stretching into the circle of light. The third man had sprung to his feet and gaped at me, his eyes shocked in a high-coloured handsome face.

For that one instant I saw them and then Yang padded up beside me. 'Please to excuse me. Missy Melody is very grieved to see the body of her father.'

They moved then, the tableau dissolving into movement and exclamation.

The portly man cried thickly, 'It's little Melody!'

'But she died! Little Melody died, didn't she?' the blonde girl asked urgently.

'We assumed that she died,' said the handsome man. 'We *assumed* she died!'

'Master told me to meet Missy at the station,' said Yang.

'And to dress her like that? To dress her in Silver Moon's clothes?' the elderly woman asked. Her voice was shaking and her hands trembled as she fumbled for the knitting she had dropped.

'My dear Heather, you're all thumbs!'

The man wearing the riding boots leaned forward to pick up needles and wool. I saw his face, strong-jawed with fair, greenish hair glinting dully along the high cheekbones. Then he stood up and slouched over to me, looking me up and down with a slight curl on his wide mouth.

'I'm Matthew Fletcher, your cousin,' he said, 'but don't expect me to shake hands with you. I have a strong and unpleasant certainty that your coming has just deprived me of a fortune.'

'For shame, Matthew,' the blonde girl tinkled. 'Poor Melody! To be so rudely greeted on her first evening! I am your other cousin, Cherry Fletcher. And that is Stephen, Matthew's brother, and this is my father Daniel.'

I looked in bewilderment at them, trying to fit names to faces, but they swam before my eyes and I felt abruptly so tired that I swayed a little.

'The girl needs a stiff drink,' said the elderly man, as his own hand, I noticed, clenched and unclenched around the stem of his glass.

'And you're just the person to provide it, my dear uncle,' drawled the one called Matthew.

I decided that I disliked him intensely, and the decision gave me the courage, born of anger I suppose, to fling up my head, denying my weariness.

'At least it is pleasant to find *one* member of my family, apart from the servants, who is willing to welcome me,' I said coldly.

'We are all behaving very badly,' said Stephen, with a faintly conscious charm. 'But for eighteen years we have believed you to be dead, or flourishing in Peking.'

'Is the gap so narrow between the two conditions?' I asked sharply. 'Didn't my father tell anyone where I was?'

'Not a word, but if you'd known Uncle Eben, you'd know he never willingly said anything to anybody.'

'You shouldn't speak ill of the dead!' cried the elderly woman shrilly. 'Eben was a good man.'

'Eben Fletcher was a scoundrel,' said Matthew calmly. 'Because he gave you a home after your husband died doesn't persuade me that he was a saint. It saved advertising for a nurse for Cherry.'

'That was an infamous thing to say,' she choked.

'Draw it steady, old son!' his uncle advised. 'No call to upset Heather. Yang, you old devil! Why didn't you let us know what Eben told you to do?'

'Master said to meet Missy Melody at the station and bring her in old coach, up back stairs to Madam Silver Moon's room,' Yang returned placidly. 'Missy must wear Madam's clothes and then I must bring Missy down to you at supper.'

'But I insisted on seeing my father first,' I said. 'Why didn't you tell me he was dead, Yang?'

'Master didn't tell me to say that,' he returned.

Matthew's harsh laugh broke out.

'That's the truth, I swear it!' he exclaimed. 'Yang has only room in his head for one idea at a time, and none of those is an original one. He is bound by the traditions of Old China and the Master's Orders. He respects the former and obeys the latter, come hell and high water.'

'I came to tell Missy that supper is now prepared,' Yang said. 'If Missy gives the command, we may all eat.'

'If Missy gives the—but this is intolerable!' Heather cried. 'Are we to wait for a stranger's leave before we break bread at Moonflete.'

'Yang is a trifle premature, I feel,' Stephen observed. 'After all, the will hasn't yet been read. We don't know if Melody gets it all.'

'We can make an educated guess,' said Matthew dryly. 'I can think of no other reason why Uncle Eben should keep us all dancing attendance on him for the past twenty years! '

'Oh, do let's go in and eat,' Cherry begged, coaxingly. She was in her early twenties, I guessed, but her confiding air made her seem younger.

'It's very unfeeling of you,' said Heather, 'to

think of eating when the coffin is not even closed yet!'

'Well, I, for one, don't propose to starve until after the funeral on Monday,' said Stephen, cheerfully backing his brother.

Set side by side, they were very much alike, though Matthew was slightly taller and broader. The greatest difference between them lay in their expressions. Stephen's face bore an open, honest, fiery look. Matthew's expression veered from a settled cynicism to a steady blaze of dislike.

He directed the blaze towards me now, as he observed, 'Well, shall we seek the dining room or would Melody prefer it if we waited about for Uncle Eben's resurrection?'

'Melody would like to eat. The question of resurrection is so uncertain,' I said sweetly. I had never come across anyone who showed his dislike of me so plainly, and my own antagonism leapt to meet him.

The dining room, brilliantly lit and decorated with comical, fantastic masks in a variety of brilliant colours was laid with silver and delicate porcelain. I was afraid we would have to cope with Oriental cooking, but the meal, though exquisitely cooked and served, was pure English—a mushroom soup, veal pasties, tender roast lamb with minted peas, a dish of buttered swedes, lemon tart and thick slices of a rich, dark cake heavy with plums and nuts. With the meal came a variety of red and white wines and a deep bowl of frosted grapes.

The men ate heartily but the two ladies picked at the various courses. They were served by Yang who moved silently from place to place, always attending me first. He had motioned me to the head of the table, to the place where I was sure Eben Fletcher had always sat. My first reaction was to move aside but the amused contempt on Matthew's face nettled me so much that I sat defiantly in the big carved chair.

Nodding at the masks around the walls, Cherry said, evidently hoping to make conversation, 'Uncle Eben brought those back from China. They wear them at festivals and funerals to scare away the evil spirits. He brought lots of beautiful things home with him. They used to be kept at 'Jason Hall' until Moonflete was built.

'Where is Jason Hall?' I asked.

'Across the valley, above the mill.' It was Heather who answered. 'The Fletchers moved in when my father died. Before that they lived further down the valley at "Fletcher House". It's empty now; crumbling away.'

'What Heather is trying to tell you,' said Matthew, 'is that old Mr. Jason died a bankrupt and Uncle Eben stepped in and bought up the big house and the land. The old Jason property became Fletcher property. Heather stayed on in the house, as part of the transaction.'

'Eben was very kind to me,' Heather said, flushing deeply. 'He could have turned me out, but he let me stay. And now he's dead.'

Tears filled her eyes and began to roll down her cheeks.

'How did he die?' I took the opportunity of asking.

'He had a heart attack, yesterday,' Stephen said. 'He was past seventy, you know, and the doctor had warned him against too much rich food, over-excitement, all that sort of thing.'

'What caused it?' I enquired.

'Nothing in particular. He was right as rain an hour earlier. Then Cherry heard a crash from his room and went in and found him on the floor.'

'It was awful!' Cherry said. 'He kept clutching at his chest and twisting about and moaning something—'

'I didn't know he'd spoken,' said her father, sharply. 'You didn't tell me that he'd spoken.'

'I forgot about it until this minute,' Cherry said. 'Anyway it didn't make much sense. Something about moonstones.'

In that moment I felt danger, as tangible as a cold draught on the back of my neck. But one can rise and seek the ill-fitting window and eliminate the annoyance. I could not pinpoint the source of the danger. I only knew that it existed and that the guileless phrase 'I have a moonstone necklace,' shrivelled in my mouth.

'Moonstones?' said Heather. 'I don't recall any moonstones in the house.'

'Eben never bothered too much about jewellery,' Daniel rumbled.

'I ran for help and Matthew rode over for the doctor, but poor Uncle Eben died a few seconds after I found him,' Cherry said sadly.

'You and my father were brothers?' I asked Daniel.

He nodded, draining the liquid in the glass and signalling impatiently for the decanter.

'There were three of us, Eben, Tom and me,' he said genially. 'There were sixteen years between Eben and me. Tom and Kate—he married one of the Wheelwright girls—were both killed in a coach accident back in 'thirty-seven. Matthew was eleven then; Stephen ten.'

'And Eben took care of them, paid for their education, gave them everything they wanted,' Heather said.

'And Cherry is your daughter?' I asked him.

'My little Cherry!' He gave her a moistly sentimental look. 'Her mother died when she was born. My wife was one of the Frazer sisters. They used to call them the Valley Graces. Sarah, Mollie and Jane. Sarah and Molly died young, but I wed Jane. And she died.'

'But you have me, father,' Cherry pouted.

'Yes, indeed. My little Cherry!' he cried.

'You know it's at times like these that I am absolutely delighted that Stephen and I lost both parents in one fell swoop,' Matthew drawled.

'That's a terrible thing to say,' Heather cried plaintively. 'Your parents' deaths were a tragedy.'

'What did my father do?' I asked, trying to forestall what threatened to become another argument.

'To earn his money, do you mean?' Stephen cocked an eyebrow.

'The Fletchers were merchants and cotton manufacturers,' said Heather.

'Were?'

'Still are,' said Matthew coldly. 'The mill will open again, I assure you.'

'Uncle Eben let the mill run down,' said Cherry. 'He had so much money that he could afford to retire, you see.'

'Thereby throwing an entire village out of work,' said Matthew. 'Jason was a flourishing place when I was a boy. My father was interested in the mill and concerned about the people. After he was killed, the business ran down. But things will change.'

'Matthew hoped to use his share of the inheritance from Uncle Eben to open up the mill again,' Cherry explained.

'Sheer waste of time!' Daniel exclaimed.

'Since the war between the American States began, there's been a blockade on raw cotton imported to Lancashire,' Stephen told me. 'It's a voluntary blockade. So if Matthew did re-open the mill, he'd have neither raw materials nor workers. Uncle Daniel is right.'

'The Americans won't fight for ever,' Matthew declared. 'Even if the war lasted for another year or two, then the blockade wouldn't bother me. Eben Fletcher didn't get in all his cotton from the States.'

'From where did he get it?' I asked.

'From China,' said Matthew. 'He owned two clipper boats and they made the China run every year, and brought back the finest and cheapest cotton.'

His grey eyes had lost their cynical, indifferent look and his face was eager.

'So you propose to go sailing?' Uncle Daniel's voice was wry. 'The old disease has broken out in the Fletcher clan again.'

'What disease?' I enquired.

'Wanderlust!' said Uncle Daniel. 'We were seafarers in our grandfather's time. My brother Eben was rich enough to buy out the Jasons and take over the mill after Heather's father died. But his ships always interested him more than cotton. He put Tom in charge of the business and sailed with his ships. Up to twenty years ago, even though Tom was dead, Eben was never here.'

'But he did come home?'

'He came home from his last voyage twenty years ago,' said Matthew. 'He came home with his bride, with Silver Moon. They'd met and married in Peking. God knows how he managed to get into the city or out of it alive. We'd been officially at war with China for some time and foreigners were hated. But the old scoundrel managed it and got himself a wife.'

'But he must have been quite old!' I exclaimed.

'Past fifty,' said Stephen. 'Silver Moon was eighteen. Yang and Astra arrived with her. She'd learned a little English, but in the two years she was here, she learned to chatter almost fluently.'

'Two years? Then she died when I was born.'

I felt sympathy for the foreign bride brought to this strange new land.

'Eben sold his ships and built Moonflete,' said Heather. 'In six months the house was built and furnished. An army of workmen were called in. You could hear the hammering clear across the valley.'

'He brought Silver Moon here, and the rest of us came too—except for Heather,' said Stephen.

'I was just married and Eben gave me back the deeds to Jason House,' said Heather. 'My old home, given back to me! It was a miracle. Cherry was just a baby, so I kept her with me as her own mother, Jane, had just died. I'll hear nothing against Eben.'

She gave us a defiant, tearful stare and a toss of her head.

'And Silver Moon died? How did she die?' I asked, and felt again that draught of danger as if something or somebody in the room quivered and warned.

'We don't know how she died,' Uncle Daniel said. 'We don't even know if she did!'

'Of course she's dead,' Stephen said impatiently. 'After eighteen years she couldn't still be alive.'

'We thought Melody was dead,' said Matthew. 'You both vanished together.'

He made the statement so coldly that for an instant the sense of it simply didn't register. Then I realised that they were all looking at me, waiting for me to react in some way.

I wondered wildly if there was an accepted code of conduct to be followed when one heard that one's mother had vanished. If there was, Miss Trimlett had never informed me of it, and not knowing how to behave, not at this moment even feeling deeply involved in the fate of a virtual stranger, I simply stared back at him.

His mouth curled again and he repeated, 'You both vanished on the same day.'

'You mean that my mother simply disappeared?'

'Like smoke.' Uncle Daniel gave a queer little laugh. 'Faded and failed into the air, as they say.'

'Leaving Moonflete and my uncle and everything else behind,' Stephen added.

There was an odd, satisfied note in his voice and I glanced at him, puzzled.

'She was happy here,' said Uncle Daniel. 'We all liked her. She was very happy.'

'She was afraid,' Heather said. 'In those last weeks, after Melody was born, she was very troubled. I sensed it; so did Eben, for he asked me if I knew what was wrong.'

'Then she ran away, and took me with her.' I stopped, remembering that my father had known where to find me.

'That's impossible,' said Matthew. 'Silver Moon could never have run away.'

'But if she was unhappy?'

'She could never have run away, because she couldn't walk properly,' said Matthew. 'Her feet were bound. It's the custom with high-born Chinese girls. Silver Moon could scarcely hobble from one room to the next. So she could never have gone anywhere of her own free will.'

CHAPTER FOUR

That night, clad in a lace-trimmed gown that had once belonged to my mother, I slept in my mother's room. Whenever I stirred and opened my eyes, the whiteness of the room glimmered against the blackness revealed by the half-drawn curtains. I woke often during that night, tossing and turning in the wide, beautiful bed. Had Silver Moon also lain wakeful eighteen years before? Had she too seen the inky darkness beyond the window and heard wind howling across the moors?

It was broad daylight when I awoke and a tap at the door admitted Astra who came in with a tray on which breakfast was laid. I saw her eyes flicker at once to the cabinet where I had put the necklace, and the look of terror shadowed her old face.

'The necklace is beautiful, isn't it?' I said deliberately.

Her eyes met mine and the blandness returned to her expression as if somebody had passed a sponge over her face.

'It was given to me on my eighteenth birthday, left in the garden of my London home,' I said. 'Was it my mother's?'

'My eyes are old. I cannot see very clearly, Missy Melody. If you will pardon me, I must make ready your bath,' she said tonelessly, and went through into the inner room. I was startled a moment later to hear Yang's voice within, but when I pulled on a robe and went to investigate, I found the door that had been locked the previous night now stood open and Yang was climbing up a flight of outside steps with two large pails dangling from his bony wrists.

'Yang brings up hot water every day from the kitchens for Madam Silver Moon,' said

Astra. 'Now he will bring it for you.'

'After eighteen years the water grows heavier,' Yang puffed as he emptied the water into the sunken bath.

My first impulse was to tell him not to tire himself, but there was a pride in his old face that made me hold my tongue.

Instead I went back into the bedroom, followed by Astra, who began to light the fire. I sat down on the rumpled bed and began to eat my breakfast, but the thought of that door leading to the outside staircase bothered me.

'Who has keys to the door in there?' I asked abruptly. 'It was locked yesterday.'

'There is a key in the kitchen, Missy, and another key here.' She opened a little drawer in the wall and showed me a neat row of keys. 'You see, Missy, the key to the stair-door, the key to the bathroom, the key to this room. And the keys here to the cupboards. But Madam locked only the stair-door.'

'And in the morning Yang unlocks it with the key from the kitchen, and brings up the water?'

'Yes, Missy.'

'And is the kitchen locked?'

'Yes, Missy. In these days it is locked up at night.'

'In these days? You mean that it wasn't locked when my mother lived here?'

'No, Missy. Who would steal from a kitchen?'

'Then why is it locked now?'

'Bad times now, Missy. Our houses are no longer safe.'

She was interrupted by Yang who called to her from the bathroom, presumably to tell her the bath was ready though he spoke in a high, sing-song gibberish.

'It would be better, Missy,' Astra said, 'if you did not wear—*that*.' She nodded towards the moonstones. 'It would be better if I put it away safely in the cabinet.'

Beneath her quiet tone was a desperation I recognised without understanding. After a moment I nodded and she fairly scurried to put the necklace into the cabinet. But her face was drawn with more than age when she turned again.

The leisurely bath, with the outer door now closed, the ministrations of the old Chinese woman, the slim skirted dress of amber velvet with a matching cloak and hood, made me feel cherished as I had never been in my life before. And in these unfashionable but beautiful garments I still looked lovely, even after a troubled night.

When I was ready, Astra said, 'The church begins at eleven, Missy will find the little carriage comfortable.'

I followed her along the corridor and down the wide stairs into a large entrance hall. I had excused myself after supper last night and come up to my room, leaving the Fletchers

44

to discuss the astonishing change in their circumstances. Now they awaited me in the hall, the two ladies in black again.

'Perhaps I should have worn mourning,' I hesitated.

'I can't think why you should consider it necessary,' Matthew said in his insolent, casual way. 'You never knew Eben Fletcher, and, in any event, I understand the Chinese don't wear black as a sign of grief, only white at the actual funeral.'

'Thank you. You must teach me more about the customs of my ancestors, since I assume you have studied them so carefully,' I said sweetly.

'*Touché*!' said Matthew, and grinned so suddenly and disarmingly that I almost smiled back.

'Did you sleep well?' Cherry asked politely.

'I woke once or twice,' I admitted.

'We are all staying at Moonflete at the moment,' she explained, taking my arm in a friendly manner as we went to the front of the house where a smart gig awaited us on the sweep of gravel.

'I thought that you all lived here all the time,' I said.

'Frank and I divide our time between Moonflete and our own home at Jason Hall,' said Heather. In contrast to Cherry her manner was stiff and wary.

'Frank?'

'My son, Francis Jason Broome. He is staying with some friends in Rochdale at the moment, but he will be here for the funeral tomorrow.'

'The family would be inconsolable if he didn't arrive,' Matthew observed, swinging his leg over the saddle of his horse.

In the gig, I turned to look at Moonflete. Its size astonished me, for its white walls seemed to crown the sloping moor, dominating the landscape. I had approached it, I realised, from the back, across the deep valley and up the hill. In front of the house the moors encroached upon the gravel path, and the path became a wider track leading down towards a huddle of houses.

'Fletchers have been climbing in Jason since my grandfather's time,' Matthew said, leaning to speak to me as we set off. 'Right at the foot of the hill in the village is the Fletcher House. It's a ruin now but Uncle Eben brought up his three sons there and made enough money to enable his son to buy the Jason property higher up the hill. And twenty years later he built Moonflete.'

'At the top of the hill,' I said, and tried to feel some affinity with my father's people who had, in two generations, risen so high.

We reached the village, a silent place of huddled houses and treacherous cobbles with a few bow-windowed shops and a green with rusting stocks. The few people we passed were

46

in their Sabbath best, but that best was darned and patched and their faces were tired and apathetic. Stephen, riding alongside the gig, gestured towards the blackened chimneys of some ugly buildings set back from the main road.

'That's the mill,' he told me. 'It ran down gradually but we kept it going up to about ten years ago. Since then most of the villagers have found work elsewhere or tried to strike out on their own. Now, with the blockade on American cotton, they're near starving. And they won't take charity.'

'They would have taken it from my father, from a Jason,' Heather said.

'Old Jason gave away so much that in the end he was bankrupt,' Uncle Daniel said.

Mounted, like his nephews, on a handsome horse, he looked glossy and well-fed as his beast. I hated his smugness, his lack of concern for the people who drifted past us, hungry, shabby and proud. At least Matthew for all his unpleasantness had wanted to open up the mill again.

We stopped before a large church with a railed cemetery at the side. Heather descended from the gig with some difficulty. I noticed that this morning she carried a silver-topped walking stick, and in the gap between sleeve and glove her wrist-joints swelled.

'Rheumatism!' she said briefly, catching my glance. 'The doctor said that I must spend my

47

winters in a warmer climate. Eben was going to arrange it.' Unspoken were the words, But now he is dead and I don't know if I will be able to afford such a luxury.

I heard very little of the service, was barely conscious of the whispers that greeted my arrival as the members of the congregation leaned forward to watch me. Instead my thoughts ran on, despite my attempts to concentrate, down a road that led me to fear and suspicion.

Eighteen years before, my Chinese mother had vanished without a trace, from a beautiful home and an evidently adoring husband. She had vanished though her feet were bound too tightly for her to do more than hobble. And I had disappeared at the same time. My father had known of my whereabouts, had kept them secret from his relatives, and had arranged when I was of Silver Moon's age to bring me back to the house, dressed in Silver Moon's clothes, and present me to the family. It all added up to one thing. Eben Fletcher knew or suspected that his young wife had been killed. Fearful for my safety he had spirited me to London, giving out that we had both vanished at the same time, and then he had waited until he could produce the replica, hoping that the killer would be startled into some confession.

That first tableau sprang to my mind— Heather, needles dropped and hands upraised, and revulsion on her face. But Heather was no relative; there was no reason for her to hate Silver Moon. It would have been more logical for her to hate Eben Fletcher who had bought her family home, yet she spoke of him with unmistakable gratitude.

Daniel? As his brother's heir, Daniel had had more reason than anybody to fear Eben's marriage. Eighteen years before, Daniel would have been about thirty-six, married with a tiny daughter whom he obviously adored. Had Daniel rid Moonflete of its occupant for the sake of his motherless child? It was hard to imagine such violence in the stout, red-faced man, but one never knew.

And Uncle Daniel had not been the only one who had hoped to benefit from Eben's will. I remembered Matthew's sardonic, 'Your coming has deprived me of a fortune,' his plans for re-opening the mill, his obvious dislike of me. Eighteen years before, Matthew had been sixteen. At sixteen passions can run high. And what of Stephen who had been only a year younger? Stephen who was so charming, so eager to welcome me?

The service was over and we were coming out into the flag-stoned porch. The minister, whose name I didn't catch, was shaking hands with me and murmuring condolences. He was a young man and presumably hadn't heard any local gossip, for his greeting was incurious. Several people, however, stopped to stare at me.

I was glad when we got back to our places in the gig and started up the hill again. I had not yet seen the old Fletcher place, but Cherry pointed towards a large building surrounded by trees and set back from the road.

'That's Jason Hall. Heather lives there,' she told me.

I noted that she didn't bestow upon the older woman the courtesy title of 'aunt'. Yet Heather had brought her up after her own mother's death.

On an impulse I asked, 'Do you remember my mother, Cherry? Do you remember anything of her?'

'Heavens, how could I? I was only three when she died,' she exclaimed.

'I thought she vanished.'

'She did, just as you did, but everyone spoke of her as dead,' Cherry explained. Then her blue eyes widened. 'You came back. Wouldn't it be odd if Silver Moon came back too!'

Heather suddenly lashed the horses with her whip and they bounded forward, digging up small stones that flew about the wheels of the gig. Her face within its black mourning bonnet was grimly set, her swollen wrists tense on the reins.

'Steady there!' Uncle Daniel called from behind. 'You'll overturn if you're not careful.'

'That's how Matthew and Stephen's parents were killed,' said Cherry. 'It was before I was born of course; but the horses bolted and

Uncle Tom and Aunt Kate were thrown out and killed. Heather took care of the boys then. Uncle Eben didn't allow them to go away to school, though I think they had a tutor for a little while.'

The picture of my father, whom I had seen for the first and last time lying in his coffin, was becoming clearer. Eben Fletcher had been a strong-willed, ambitious man, with a great love of beauty and a generous streak in his nature. He had given Heather a place in the Fletcher circle, had handed back her old home to her as a wedding gift. He had brought up his two nephews, and as far as I could tell, Uncle Daniel and Cherry had always lived at his expense. Yet for eighteen years he had bided his time, waiting for the moment when he could trap a killer. A man of strong will, I thought, and vengeful heart. I could not have borne to live so long with people of whom I could suspect such a thing.

We had reached the big white house again. It seemed, somehow, typical of my father that he had made no attempt to plant a garden around his home. The white stone sprang up defiantly from the moor, saying quite clearly, Here I am, built by a Fletcher who began his life at the bottom of the hill. Within, I hold unimaginable riches, but the uninvited must gaze from afar.

The front door stood open as we descended from the gig, and a groom hurried to lead the horses round to the stables; a young man, of my own age or a little older, ran lightly down the steps towards us.

'Mother, I'm back!' he called, announcing the fact with a mocking insouciance that parodied the image of a returning son.

So this, I thought, was Francis, the son of Heather. He was very handsome—not tall, but slim and graceful, with auburn hair and the clear, transparent complexion that sometimes goes with it. But there was nothing effeminate in him despite long lashes and tapering fingers.

'The servants told me that Cousin Melody had come back!' he exclaimed.

'Not your cousin!' Cherry said, rudely and loudly.

'Forgive me, but I always think of the Fletchers as my relatives. My father died when I was a baby. Uncle Eben brought me up.'

'He's dead. Eben is dead,' Heather said bleakly. 'And now that Cousin Melody has come back I don't know what is to become of us.'

'Don't fret, Mother. We'll be perfectly all right.'

He put his arm round her shoulders and gave me a quick, crooked smile.

'The old gentleman had a bad heart,' he said. 'He had several turns last summer, so we really expected it to end like this. But mother and I were very fond of him and grateful for his kindnesses, so naturally she has taken it very hard.'

'Cheer up! You may still come in for a small legacy when the will is read,' Matthew said dryly.

'That was unnecessary,' I began, but the boy smiled and gave a little shake of his head.

'Matthew is always in a bad humour on Sundays,' he said, lightly. 'The sermon gives him indigestion, I believe. I am Francis Broome, by the way. I have a feeling that you have been told about me already.'

'Not very much,' I said.

'Well, don't ask my mother. She is too apt to give you a recital of all my virtues and leave you to discover only my faults,' he said.

'And I will tell you all his faults and join in the search for his virtues,' Matthew said.

'You must tell me all about yourself, then I will have a balanced picture,' I said coolly.

'Have you seen Uncle Eben?' Heather asked. 'He looked very peaceful.'

'I did go into the library but the coffin was closed.'

I was glad to hear it. The picture of my father lying there, his nose jutting to the ceiling, had been one of the images that had disturbed my sleep.

As we went into the house Cherry came up beside me, plucking at my cloak.

'What do you think of Frank?' she whispered. 'I can't bear him. We none of us can! But Uncle Eben spoiled him. I suppose because his father died. Well, my mother died when I was born and he never spoiled me!'

Heather had paused at the foot of the stairs and said, in a voice raised for my benefit, 'I had hoped that Frank and I could stay at Moonflete until after the funeral. But as everybody seems to take it for granted that Melody is now the owner—'

'Of course you must both stay,' I began impulsively, but Matthew cut in sharply.

'Until the will is read I assume that the house belongs to Uncle Daniel who is next-of-kin.'

'But I thought a daughter was next-of-kin,' I protested. 'The law says—'

'We must have a long talk about the law some time,' Matthew said genially, and raked me with a cold, unpleasant stare.

CHAPTER FIVE

The morning of my father's funeral was sunny and mild, with a faint blue haze over the hills. I had spent the previous day in a series of aimless conversations with Cherry who wanted to know all about the London fashions, and with Frank who was bursting with curiosity about me and the years in which I had been hidden. His curiosity must have outweighed the grief he felt at his patron's death, for he had thrown off his shock with all the ease of a volatile nature, and talked freely of his own expectations.

I encouraged him to talk, for it was clear to me that only by listening carefully could I hope to begin to know this strange assortment of people. Often, with only Miss Trimlett for company, I had longed for the lively society of people my own age.

Now I sat in a flower-papered parlour with a handsome young man, and all the time I must remember that he was the son of a woman who had obviously hated my mother.

I must try to watch as well as listen, to note the pauses between some words, the emphasis on others, to suspect guilt where there might only be pure friendliness.

'I did think that Uncle Eben—I always called him that—might leave something for my mother. Perhaps it was unrealistic of me. You know that he gave mother the deeds to her old home on her wedding day? Unhappily, he gave her no money with which to pay her bills. But she spends most of her time at Moonflete, anyway. And I received the same education as Matthew and Stephen, though they despise me for it.'

'They ought not to despise you,' I said crossly.

'One can't blame them,' Frank said tolerantly. 'After all, they were his real nephews. I had, and still have, no claim on his

55

kindness at all. Perhaps if he had apprenticed me to some trade, instead of bringing me up to a gentleman's life—'

He smiled ruefully and spread his hands.

'Matthew and Stephen don't do anything either, and they're in their mid-thirties,' I pointed out.

'They both worked in the mill, carried out all the business, until Uncle Eben lost interest in it and turned off the workers. By then it was too late for them to change, and they had no money.'

So my father had been a tyrant, kindly in many ways perhaps, but still a tyrant, making it impossible for any of his dependents to leave him. And they had stayed, patiently waiting for their share of the inheritance.

And among those who waited was the one who had killed Silver Moon. Killed her perhaps as she lay in her big white bed. Creeping up the outside stair with the key from the kitchen and then—? My mind closed against the possibility of what had happened next.

But before going to bed that night I went into the kitchen where Astra was preparing meat for the next day, and asked her for the key.

'Yes, Missy Melody.'

She bowed, dusted her hands on her apron and took down the key from a row of hooks on the wall.

'Astra, why is the house locked up at night, nowadays?' I asked. 'Is it since Silver Moon—went?'

'No, Missy. For a year only when bad men begin to move across the moors. Since then we lock up the door to the kitchen.'

'Bad men? What bad men?'

'I do not know their names,' she said, 'and their faces are hidden. But they are very bad men.'

I wanted to question her. I wanted to question everybody, but each question seemed to reveal another question. And I was not even sure if I could trust Astra. She was a foreigner to me.

Despite my half-Chinese blood, I had been reared as an English girl, with no knowledge of my ancestors. I had never tried to find out about China or the people of that land, had turned away my head on the rare occasions we saw some Oriental in the street for fear somebody might notice my own yellow skin.

I wished that I could tell how Astra's mind worked, what lay behind her respectful manner, her soft lilting voice.

'Will Missy need my services?' she asked now. 'I will lay out the mourning dress in time for tomorrow. I must slice the meat and slice the onions and mix the cake. With my old hands I must prepare the food for the Master's funeral day.'

I had left her to her proud, sad task and

gone back to Cherry and her London talk. Chattering to my cousin who seemed to admire and like me was preferable to wandering through the great house. I longed to explore Moonflete, for every room was filled with fantastic and beautiful objects.

Matthew watched me finger a delicate vase.

'Finding out the value of your property?' he observed sardonically.

After that I stayed in one place, and took care not to look for too long at anything.

But a seed of covetedness sprang up in me. This was a lovely, lovely house. Surely my father would not have left too much of his property to Uncle Daniel who, good-natured as he seemed, had been drinking steadily ever since we returned from church.

On the morning of my father's funeral, I stood, wrapped in a white cloak, isolated from the black dresses of Heather and Cherry and the dark, mourning suits of Uncle Daniel, Matthew, Stephen and Frank.

There were one or two people standing about at the cemetery gates and a few more around the open grave, but it struck me forcibly that none of the villagers had attended. Yet Eben Fletcher had been the richest man in the district.

I guessed that after his closure of the mill the people of Jason had resented him so much that they would not even pay him the tribute of attending his funeral. The thought of it caused me deep sadness, for something in me cried out that it was wrong for any man to go unmourned to his grave.

No, not completely unmourned. Heather was weeping bitterly into her handkerchief, and the men stood with bowed heads. Cherry had covered her rosy, pretty face with a black veil, to hide her tears, or the lack of them? I could not tell, because I was a stranger here, among relatives I had never known.

An elderly man wearing gold-rimmed spectacles was among the mourners. He had arrived late and I saw him look at me before he gave his attention to the ritual. I wondered if this might be Briggs, and my supposition was confirmed when the final Amen had been intoned and we were moving away from the graveside.

'Miss Melody Fletcher? I am your late father's lawyer,' he began, coming over to me with quick, neat little steps.

'Mr. Briggs? Miss Trimlett mentioned your name.'

'I had the pleasure of interviewing the lady some fifteen years ago,' he nodded. 'A most charming person. You have been happy with her?'

'Very happy.'

I shook hands politely and turned to introduce the others, but Mr. Briggs was already making himself known to them.

'Mr. Daniel Fletcher? My condolences to

you, sir. Mrs. Broome, we met briefly many years ago on the occasion of your marriage.'

'And wrote very kindly to me when my husband passed away,' Heather said.

'And this will be your son, Mr. Francis Broome? A great comfort to a mother's heart, I imagine. Mr. Matthew, I am happy to meet you, though I could wish it were not in such sad circumstances. I had a very great shock when the news reached me.'

'In London?'

'Manchester, Miss Melody. I reside in the northern metropolis, but I occasionally visit London.'

'Is this the first time you've ever been to Moonflete?' I asked. 'I assumed that you would know it well.'

'I visited the place briefly when Mrs. Broome was married. It had only just been built at that time. But Mr. Eben Fletcher was a man who preferred to keep his home life quite separate from his legal and business affairs.'

'A secretive man?' I hazarded.

'Perhaps a little too secretive.' Mr. Briggs glanced back through the gates as he assisted me to the carriage. 'We ought not to speak ill of the dead, and I have always had the greatest respect for your father, but he did sometimes seem to relish the very flavour of intrigue.'

'May we offer you a lift up to the house?' I enquired.

'That won't be necessary, thank you. I hired

a cab to bring me here, so I'll use it as far as the house, and perhaps beg alternative transport on the way home. I judged it better as I was a trifle late to break my journey at the church.'

He bowed and trotted across the road to where a cab waited.

We were travelling in a black coach with black ribbon tied to the reins. I had not seen either Yang or Astra at the funeral which surprised me a little.

From her seat opposite, Heather spoke disturbing my thoughts.

'There were very few people there to pay their last respects. One would have thought—'

Her voice trailed away into a doleful murmur.

'I do think it was brave of you to wear white,' Cherry said admiringly, putting back her veil and revealing a face innocent of tearstains. 'I know it's the Chinese custom, but *in* Lancashire . . .'

'It gave me quite a turn,' said Heather. 'Watching you was like watching Silver Moon come back to see them put Eben in his grave.'

'I am not Silver Moon,' I said.

'No, my dear. I'm quite aware of that,' she said, mildly reproving.

'Is Mr. Briggs going to read the will straight after dinner?' Cherry enquired.

'I'm sure I don't know. I'm not a member of the family,' Heather said.

Some weakness in me, born of pity I suppose, made me say, 'Heather, if I may call you that, I do hope that you will regard yourself as a member of the family while I am at Moonflete.'

Heather's eyes flickered as if she sought to veil some emotion that she wished to keep hidden. Then she leaned forward, putting her gloved hand on mine.

'You have a great deal of your father's kindness in you. Frank and I will never forget what we owe to him.'

At that instant through the drawn blinds of the carriage came a series of bangs, shrieks and ear-splitting yells so out of tune with the mood of the moment that we all three stared at one another, appalled. But, as the vehicle stopped and we alighted, to join the gentlemen who were just dismounting, Uncle Daniel rumbled at us.

'It's Yang and Astra! Believe they can frighten away spirits by clashing pan handles together. Heathenish rubbish!'

'Do you think they'll keep it up during dinner?' Cherry giggled.

'I hope not. Will somebody please tell them that Missy Melody would like them to stop!' I exclaimed.

'You give orders so fluently that one might imagine you'd been practising,' Matthew drawled.

I ignored him and went to meet Mr. Briggs

who had paid off the cab and came tripping towards us, rubbing his hands together as he observed that the wind seemed to be freshening a trifle.

We talked commonplaces throughout the dinner, but while I made the right responses and admired the lawyer's fluent and tactful small talk, I was conscious of impatience within myself and within those who sat round the table. We were all waiting for the moment when Mr. Briggs would read the will, for the moment when some part of my father's strange, secretive behaviour might be explained.

'If we are all ready, shall we go into one of the other rooms?' Mr. Briggs hinted.

'The garden room, I think.'

It was Uncle Daniel who made the suggestion. He might, after all, be the new master of Moonflete.

We went into the room where I had first seen them all together. Now I sat amongst them in a semi-circle of chairs and Mr. Briggs seated himself behind a small table and drew several papers from a briefcase he had been keeping by his side during dinner.

'Mr. Briggs, can you tell me anything?' I asked. 'Until two days ago I didn't know anything of my father or his family. I'd never heard of Moonflete. I received a letter, apparently written to the bank and sent on, telling me to come up here.'

'I can tell you very little,' he said, lifting his hands and letting them fall to the documents on the table again. 'I was engaged almost eighteen years ago—seventeen years and seven months, to be exact—by Mr. Eben Fletcher. He informed me that his wife, Silver Moon, who was a lady of Chinese birth, had disappeared a fortnight earlier in circumstances which he described as suspicious. He had immediately despatched a lady called Mrs. Ackers—'

'Her husband was overseer at the mill,' Uncle Daniel exclaimed. 'He died of the typhus the previous year.'

'The lady was, I understand, a widow,' said Mr. Briggs, with a faint inflection of reproof in his voice, for the interruption. 'The lady had Mr. Fletcher's small baby with her, a girl called Melody. Mr. Fletcher told me that he had sent the child out of his house a few hours after discovering his wife's absence. He instructed me to engage a governess and staff and install them in a respectable house, in the greatest possible secrecy. After that I was to arrange for regular drafts to be paid into a London bank.'

'And you just accepted all this!' Stephen exclaimed.

'I advised him most strongly against it,' the lawyer said stiffly. 'I pointed out that if he had reason to suspect that some person had harmed his wife and constituted a threat to his child, then he should inform the authorities.'

'And what did he say to that?' Uncle Daniel asked. His hands gripped each other tensely.

'He said that he was quite capable of dealing with trouble inside his own family,' Mr. Briggs said.

'His own family? That sounds as if he suspected that one of us had—'

'Killed Silver Moon? Why don't you say it, Heather?' Matthew's indolent tone was lively with contempt. 'We've all been thinking it. All these years we've eyed one another, wondering who killed Silver Moon, and how and where is the body. More than that, for we all thought Melody was dead too—all of us except *one!*'

'As I was about a year old at the time my conscience is clear,' Frank said airily.

'As you're not a Fletcher I'd advise you to keep quiet!' Stephen said.

'My father arranged for me to be brought back here, dressed as my mother, and presented to the family in the hope the murderer would confess,' I said breathlessly. 'It went wrong because my father died.'

'It was too late to prevent your arrival,' Mr. Briggs said. 'Mr. Fletcher had previously informed me of his intention to bring you home, though not of his motive.'

'Hadn't we better get to the will?' Uncle Daniel asked.

'Mr. Fletcher drafted this will a year ago,' Mr. Briggs said. 'I told him quite frankly that I thought its terms were quite scandalous.

65

Unfortunately they are completely legal and Mr. Fletcher was not, at the time of making them, or as far as I know at any time since, anything but completely healthy in mind and body.'

'For God's sake, read it,' Stephen muttered, his tone less pleasant than usual.

'There are the usual preliminaries,' Mr. Briggs said, 'but it might be preferable for me to come at once to the main part, if that is satisfactory to you all.'

Taking silence for agreement he cleared his throat and began to read from the papers.

'To my brother Daniel Fletcher, to my nephews Matthew Fletcher and Stephen Fletcher, to my niece Charity Fletcher, to my friend Heather Broome and her son, Francis Jason Broome, I leave the sum of one thousand pounds each.

'To my daughter, Melody Fletcher, I leave the remainder and residue of my estate and possessions on condition that the said Melody Fletcher is still alive and living at Moonflete three weeks after my death. In the event of this condition not being fulfilled, the remainder and residue of my estate and possessions are to be sold at public auction and the proceeds divided equally between the aforementioned legatees.'

Mr. Briggs looked up from the paper.

'The servants, Yang and Astra receive the sum of five hundred pounds each, the other members of staff sums ranging from fifty to two hundred pounds according to the length of service. I must also tell you that Mr. Fletcher informed me of his intention of making a new will after his daughter's arrival.'

'He thought he would know the killer's name by then,' Frank murmured.

'One thousand pounds. One thousand pounds!' Uncle Daniel thumped the arm of his chair. 'And the rest to a girl we never knew still existed.'

'But not for three weeks,' said Frank, his eyes bright and amused. 'If Melody dies or disappears from Moonflete within the next three weeks we all share the money. I wonder how much it would bring.'

'Even with the present financial slump and at auction prices at least three or four hundred thousand pounds, judging from the last inventory I received,' Mr. Briggs calculated.

'It's an invitation to murder,' Heather said softly.

Nobody said anything for a moment. Then Cherry observed in her sweet, clear voice, 'Uncle Eben must have hated Melody to bring her into such a trap! If I were you, Melody, I'd be afraid, very much afraid!'

CHAPTER SIX

'He must have been insane!' Stephen exclaimed.

There was an unhappy little silence.

'I forbid you to say such a thing! I cannot—will not—sit here and listen while Eben's memory is insulted. I will not allow it,' Heather said, in a trembling voice.

'You'd do better to keep out of it,' Matthew said heartlessly. 'After all, you're hardly an expert on the analysis of character.'

'Do we have to be so unpleasant?' Frank began, flushing deeply, but Cherry broke in, her own cheeks scarlet.

'Speak for yourself, Frank Broome,' she said. 'At least the rest of us are *honestly* unpleasant. We don't smile and smirk and pretend to be what we're not!'

'All this may be highly diverting for Mr. Briggs,' Matthew yawned, 'but it hardly solves the problem.'

'I don't see why there should be a problem,' Stephen said, slowly. 'Because Uncle Eben set Melody up as bait for a killer doesn't necessarily mean she's going to be murdered. It would be so foolish to imagine that one of us is getting ready to kill her just because Silver Moon vanished.'

'But she *did* vanish!' Cherry breathed.

I felt the coldness again at the back of my neck, the lurking danger. In a vain attempt to banish it, perhaps to display some coolness in the face of danger, I said loudly, 'I agree with Stephen. My father's motives cannot alter the facts.'

'And the facts are,' drawled Matthew, 'that cousin Melody stands an excellent chance of becoming one of the richest corpses in England!'

Mr. Briggs, looking acutely uncomfortable, was glancing at his pocket-watch. I felt sorry for the little lawyer, thrust into a situation that obviously appalled him.

Stephen evidently felt the same way, for he rose.

'You'll be wanting to get back,' he said pleasantly. 'I'll see about transport for you.'

The tension was dissipated slightly in the general handshaking and farewells.

The lawyer glanced at me doubtfully once or twice as if he hoped for a private word, but I kept my head high and my smile calm. Not for anything would I admit to the others that inwardly I quaked with apprehension.

No sooner had Mr. Briggs been driven away in the carriage, however, when the family exploded again, restraints thrown off and voices shrill with indignation.

'It's an intolerable situation!' Uncle Daniel cried. 'I resent the implications in that—that scandalous will. To hint that any of us are capable of murder.'

'For a share in four hundred thousand pounds I might be induced to consider it,' Matthew drawled.

'I wasn't aware that you'd need an inducement,' I said sharply. I was so frightened that my heart hammered but I was determined to maintain a tight control over my emotions.

'Why doesn't Melody share out the money *before* she gets murdered?' Cherry suggested brightly.

That idea had occurred to me too, but hearing it said by this yellow-haired girl with the guileless blue eyes gave it a different aspect.

Matthew answered for me. 'She's not the sort of person to give in to blackmail,' he said, flatly.

'And nothing is going to happen to her anyway!' said Heather. 'Don't you see? It was a challenge to the killer, and it's a challenge that can't be taken up! If anything did happen to Melody, we'd all know that one of us had done it, and we'd be forever watching one another, suspecting one another.'

'Going on as we've been going on for the past eighteen years,' said Matthew.

'And meanwhile enjoying the money,' Stephen added.

'We'd find out who did and have him arrested!' Heather cried.

'It might be a "her",' said Matthew.

70

'That's not possible,' Heather objected. 'Don't you see, if somebody killed Silver Moon then the same person will kill Melody. There wouldn't be two murderers in one family. And none of us had any reason to kill Silver Moon—except Daniel! He was Eben's next-of-kin until Eben married.'

'Are you accusing me of murder?' Uncle Daniel asked.

His voice had dropped almost to a whisper and there was a white rim about his mouth. Looking at his thick neck and fleshy hands, I was aware of the brute strength emanating from this man.

'We don't *know* that anybody has been murdered,' I said.

But I spoke out of fear, knowing that Silver Moon had not walked out of the house of her own free will; knowing in my bones and blood with an instinct deeper than reason that the girl who had been my mother was dead, victim of some silent, ruthless killer who might strike again.

'Then hadn't we better find out what did happen to Silver Moon?' Stephen asked.

His expression held a new intensity quite different from the charm he had displayed up to that moment.

'If Melody has any sense she'll turn us all out of the house and lock herself in her room for the next three weeks,' Frank said.

'And spend the rest of my life wondering

which one of you killed my mother or might be tempted to kill me?' I shook my head as I looked round at them.

'Frank and I must go back to Jason Hall,' Heather said. 'I at least have a home to call my own.'

'And a thousand pounds,' Frank reminded her. 'With my thousand added to it you should be able to afford a few winters in a warm climate.'

'Don't be silly. You will need the money to see you through University. Uncle Eben always intended that you should go,' his mother reminded him.

'To become a gentleman? Thank you, Mother, but it's not my style.'

'That's true!' Cherry said rudely, and the boy swung round on her, his handsome face flushed.

'At least I'm spared the disagreeable necessity of proposing to you for the sake of your inheritance!' he exclaimed.

'I wouldn't have *you* as a gift!' Cherry declared.

My own feelings suddenly bubbled up into a weak and futile rage.

'As this is my house and you are guests here I'd be grateful if you'd do your quarrelling elsewhere!' I said, and sat down abruptly, feeling tears at the back of my eyes.

'We're *all* guests here,' Matthew observed. 'We've been guests here, in a way, for years.

Obviously some arrangement will have to be made.'

'I'd like you to stay,' I said quickly. 'I'd like you all to stay, for the time being at least. Believe me, but I never expected this or wanted it. Moonflete is your home more than it is mine. I've no intention of asking you to make other arrangements.'

'Besides, with all of us here, under your eye, you can keep track of our doings,' Matthew said.

'That was mean of you,' Cherry pouted. 'Melody was being kind.'

'Well, I for one don't need her kindness,' Uncle Daniel said. 'I'm not one to take charity.'

'Why not? You've been living off Uncle Eben for years,' Stephen said.

'And you and your brother haven't done too badly out of him!' the older man retorted.

'We've had our keep,' said Matthew. 'It was no more than was due to us seeing we both worked in the mill without pay until Uncle Eben closed it down.'

'Wouldn't it be better to try to find out what happened to Silver Moon instead of quarrelling among ourselves?' Frank suggested.

'What is the use of raking up an old scandal?' Heather asked uneasily.

'But *I* want to know!' I said brusquely. 'I want to know exactly what happened when my mother disappeared. Why wasn't a search made? How did you find out she'd gone?'

'You can't expect us to remember details after eighteen years!' Heather exclaimed, as her hands pleated and repleated the ends of her black shawl and her eyes were afraid.

'Frank and Cherry can't. They were too tiny,' I agreed. 'But the rest of you must remember. You were *here.*'

'I wasn't here,' Heather said quickly. 'I was living at Jason Hall with Cherry and Frank in my care. My life was very retired; my husband had died the previous summer in the typhus epidemic. Frank was a posthumous child.'

'But you were here on that day,' Matthew said suddenly. 'You came up in the afternoon to show Cherry the bonfires. There was a copse at the side of the house, Melody. A pretty place but the trees were diseased— some kind of fungus—and it was decided to clear the lot and burn the rotted wood. It took us the best part of a month to clear, and on that afternoon, Heather, you brought Cherry to watch.'

'And stayed until after supper,' Uncle Daniel chimed in. 'I walked back with you and carried Cherry part of the way.'

'What did you do then?' I asked.

'Walked back to Moonflete, as far as I remember,' he shrugged.

'No, you didn't,' Stephen said. 'I was on my way upstairs to bed when you let yourself in the side door. It was after one o'clock, and I'd

74

spent hours wrestling with the monthly accounts. You'd been out all evening.'

'I probably went for a walk,' his uncle said unconvincingly.

'I put little Cherry to bed and looked in on Frank. I'd left him with the nurse,' Heather said quickly. 'Then I read or sewed a little, and went to bed.'

'You went to sleep very late then. I was passing Jason Hall at midnight and the candles were still burning,' Matthew said accusingly.

'What were you doing out at that hour yourself?' Heather demanded.

'I'd spent the evening with friends,' Matthew said curtly.

'In the "Rovers Arms" more like—you were wild in those days,' his brother grinned.

'Stephen was the quiet one,' Matthew agreed. 'Seventeen years old and Uncle Eben trusted him with the mill accounts! I was more interested in the stuff we produced. Some of the finest cotton in the world came from Fletcher's Mill in those days.'

'So Heather was at Moonflete in the afternoon,' I said slowly. 'Uncle Daniel walked back to Jason Hall with her and she sat up late reading while he went off for another walk. Matthew was with friends until midnight and Stephen was here doing some accounts. Where were Silver Moon and my father?'

'Silver Moon was in her room. She had a headache, and didn't come down for supper that day. I heard Uncle Eben calling goodnight to her. He went out to the copse to check the bonfires. They were still smouldering but there wasn't much wind so he judged it safe to leave them,' Stephen said.

'How did you know that?'

'He put his head in at the library door and told me so. He told me not to sit up too long, addling my brain with figures, said he intended to have an early night, and went to bed.'

'In the big white bedroom?'

'In his own room. Silver Moon had her own apartments. You were sleeping in a little nursery room nearby.'

'And Silver Moon disappeared during that night?'

'As far as we know. We weren't told of it until noon the next day,' Stephen said.

'But surely she was missed!'

'Silver Moon often stayed in her room until we had dinner,' Matthew said. 'I went off down to the mill very early on. I was still learning the business.'

'I slept late,' Stephen said. 'So did you, Uncle Daniel. You were still in bed when I got up.'

'And then my father told you that Silver Moon had gone?'

'He told us that you'd both gone,' Matthew said shortly. 'We made a search, but he wouldn't inform anybody in official circles.'

'Why didn't somebody insist?'

'One didn't insist where Uncle Eben was concerned,' Matthew told me. 'Remember that we were all dependent on him.'

'So any of you could have killed my mother,' I said slowly. 'Any of you could have done it.'

The knowledge that one of them *must* have done it dragged at my heart.

'But it's not possible!' Heather said shrilly. 'It's not possible!'

'It's perfectly possible,' her son said.

'But we loved Silver Moon,' Heather persisted. 'Your mother was beautiful, Melody, gentle and lovely and loved! Greatly loved! I was her dear friend.'

'Uncle Daniel didn't like her,' said Stephen. 'He never expected Uncle Eben to marry at all; he always expected that the estate would be his one day. It was a nasty shock when Uncle Eben came home from his last voyage with a Chinese wife.'

'I never grudged Eben a wife,' Uncle Daniel said heavily. 'But why an Oriental? Why fill the house with a lot of foreigners?'

'I've often wondered,' Heather said wistfully, 'if Silver Moon wasn't killed by one of those dreadful secret societies. One hears of such things!'

'Don't be more of a fool than you can help,' Matthew advised. 'Yang and Astra would have had something to say about any strange Chinamen who came wandering around. They were devoted to Silver Moon and only slightly less devoted to Uncle Eben. Believe me, but if either of them had had the least suspicion that she was in any kind of danger they'd have given their lives to protect her.'

'It doesn't look as if our questions are leading anywhere,' Frank said. 'I propose we drop the subject. If the murderer is here he'll be lying anyway.'

But it is not only the guilty who tell lies, I thought. Sometimes the innocent lie or keep silent, for a variety of reasons.

In my own room that evening, I took a sheet of paper and wrote down what I had learned or suspected. Miss Trimlett had always stressed the value of keeping one's mind tidy and uncluttered, but my own thoughts were chaotic. The one thing that everybody seemed to accept was that Silver Moon had been murdered. My father, instead of beginning an enquiry, had sent me away in the care of a village woman, hidden me for eighteen years and then arranged for me to be brought home. But he had died of a sudden heart attack and his will had made me the bait for the killer. Obviously, if my sudden arrival had not startled somebody into confession, the will would have stayed unaltered. But he had exposed me, his own daughter, to the grossest danger.

On the paper I wrote: 'Why did my father hate me?'

Silver Moon had been killed either for

money or out of hatred.

I wrote down: 'Uncle Daniel—Eben's heir until Silver Moon came. A widower with a small girl. No money or prospects of his own. Hated foreigners.'

'Matthew—resented Silver Moon? Hoped for a share in the mill?'

'Stephen—same motives?'

'Heather—hated Silver Moon, though she says she was her friend.'

Then I penned rapidly, 'All had the chance that night to kill her. One of them *must* have done so!'

As an afterthought I wrote : 'Moonstones', and put a big, black question mark beside it. Then I tore up my useless little exercise and fed it to the flames in the grate.

If I wrote down my thoughts a hundred times over I would be no nearer a solution. I would have to talk to these people, question them, listen to the shades of meaning in their voices, build up a picture of the household to which Eben Fletcher had brought his wife. And I must remember all the time that among these people stalked a killer who had murdered once and might murder again.

I went over to the window and stared out into the gloom. I could see nothing but the grass dipping down into the steep valley at the back of the great house.

My house! Again I felt within me the triumph of possession, and with it, came a feeling of defiance. Nobody, I vowed, would cheat me out of it or kill me in order to possess it. The house was mine and the land was mine, and I would keep it despite everybody.

For the first time I dimly began to understand the quality in my father that had enabled him to rise from the bottom to the top of the hill. I began also to see why he had lost interest in the mill and turned off the workers, because he felt such contempt for those who had watched him rise that it gave him pleasure, when he had made himself master, to turn and destroy them, closing the mill and turning a prosperous village into a bleak hamlet of crumbling housed and shabby people with resentment in their eyes.

In the darkness a light flickered, a sharp pinpoint of light glinting across the valley. I leaned towards the window, frowning as I watched. The point of light seemed to be flashing a definite pattern and as I tried to make some sense out of the sequence another light flashed nearer to the house. The lights continued for the space of about five minutes and then there was darkness again.

As I drew back I heard a soft step at the door, and Astra came in. 'Will Missy have something to eat before sleep?' she enquired politely.

'Those lights, Astra? Why do they blink and shimmer like that?' I demanded.

'Lights?' Her voice quavered as she came to

my side. 'I saw no lights.'

'They've gone now. But there were two of them, signalling one to the other,' I argued.

'It is better not to look,' Astra said. 'Better to lock one's doors and go quietly to sleep, Missy. These are bad times.'

'Who makes those signals? Who shines those lights?'

'The men who ride across the moors. Bad men, Missy. It is not right that a lady should concern herself with such matters.'

'With what matters, Astra?'

'Nothing to do with Moonflete,' the old woman said stolidly. 'What happens on the moors and in the houses of others is nothing to do with us. Nothing!'

'But what happens within this house *is* my concern,' I said sharply. 'You know the terms of my father's will?'

'Mr. Matthew told me that Yang and I have money now. Is that true?'

'Five hundred pounds each,' I said. 'And Moonflete will be mine if I can stay alive for the next three weeks!'

'But Missy is very young and will live for many years yet,' Astra said, innocently.

'Why should I?' I retorted harshly. 'My mother didn't!'

Then I saw the fear come back into her eyes as she bowed and moved away.

CHAPTER SEVEN

'You'll want to inspect your property, I suppose,' Matthew said the following morning when I came downstairs. 'Do you fancy a guided tour or would you prefer to wander about by yourself, waiting for a blow on the head or a stab in the back?'

'I'll wander about alone,' I said shortly. 'I'm not in need of any company.'

'Particularly mine,' he finished for me and gave the sudden, disarming grin that lightened his brooding face. A strong, raw-boned face, I thought, studying it. The question crossed my mind, Why did this man live here for so long under his uncle's domination when he is himself obviously of determined character?

'Stop looking at me like that!' he said roughly.

'Like what?'

'As if you could see through my skull into my brain,' he said sullenly.

'Look into *my* head instead!' Stephen exclaimed, laughing as he came into the room. 'You'll find nothing but pure, innocent thoughts there, I assure you.'

He stood next to his brother and smiled at me. I thought they looked like two sides of the same coin or, perhaps like two aspects of the sea. Stephen's pleasant face and smile were like tranquil water; Matthew's features like the stormier depths beneath.

'I'd like to find out something about those lights,' I said on an impulse.

'You saw lights last night?' asked Stephen, the smile fading on his face.

'How did you know it was last night?' I asked.

'Because the lights only appear at night,' Matthew said shortly. 'The day after they have appeared, some householder in the district wakes up to find his silver gone or his strongbox emptied.'

'Men who cover their faces and ride across the moors,' I repeated.

'You're quoting Astra,' Stephen said with a quirk of the lips. 'She swears she saw men on horseback with masks over their faces riding past the house a few months back.'

'But there have been robberies? Is that why Moonflete is locked up at night now?'

'Greatly to late Uncle Eben's disgust,' said Stephen. 'He couldn't bring himself to believe that anybody would ever dare to rob him. And Heather and Cherry went on and on at him until he agreed to fit locks.'

That too fitted in with the image of my father. An ambitious upstart who collected beautiful things and displayed them to the men he had ruined, contemptuously inviting them to steal if they dared.

'Don't look so serious,' said Matthew.

'Moonflete must be the only house in the neighbourhood that hasn't been burgled in the past twelve months. Your property will be quite safe.'

'But can't you find the thieves and stop them?' I asked.

The brothers exchanged glances.

Matthew shrugged. 'Times are hard in Lancashire. Why grudge the poor devils a little excitement?'

'Matthew feels a responsibility to the workers,' Stephen said, earnestly.

'Why? You didn't close down the mill!' I protested.

'I worked there. I knew the men. When they were turned off they starved or left the district to tramp the roads. I had a luxurious home.'

'Would it have done any good to have starved with them?' I asked.

Matthew's cold eyes rested on my face for a moment.

'You are indeed Eben Fletcher's daughter,' he said, and turned away.

So Matthew had hated my father and for that reason alone would dislike me, even if I had not inherited the property. It was useful to know how matters stood, so why then should I feel this deep disappointment as if somebody had shown me something infinitely valuable and then snatched it away?

'It's a surprise to see you down so early,' Stephen was saying. 'Silver Moon never came out of her room until mid-morning.'

'My name is Melody,' I said flatly. 'I am neither my mother—nor my father.'

'And what does Melody propose to do today?' Uncle Daniel enquired genially, striding into the room. He was in cloak and riding boots, I noticed, and in response to Stephen's enquiring look, he said, 'Apparently the Fleetwoods were hit last night. Esekiel brought the news when he arrived with the milk. I thought I'd ride over and see if there's anything to be done.'

'I'll come with you,' Stephen offered. 'I promised Heather to look in on them at Jason Hall.'

'And as Melody has made it clear that she doesn't wish for my company I'll join you both,' said Matthew.

Their going was a relief. Now, apart from the servants, I was alone at Moonflete for a little while. I had a perfect right to wander through the rooms, fingering the hangings and ornaments. It was a big house and would take more than a day to explore, but I had a long time, I thought; and stifled the words 'three weeks' that came into my mind.

Eben Fletcher's tastes had been exquisite— and expensive. Looking at the beautifully woven curtains, the carved ivories, the fans and masks and gleaming silver and jade, I began to wonder if Eben had chosen all these things to please his wife or if he had chosen his wife to fit into these surroundings.

I had thought of my mother as a deeply cherished woman provided with every luxury of her adoring husband. Now I began to see everything as if in a distorting mirror, so that Silver Moon shrank down into a tiny puppet and Moonflete loomed larger and larger, becoming the object my father had loved above all other things.

He had decorated it sumptuously, furnished it exquisitely, and placed my mother within it as a final ornament.

He chose his wife to match the wallpaper, I thought, and was not certain whether to laugh or cry.

Had I been more determined or unscrupulous I suppose that I would have gone into the bedrooms occupied by the other members of the family. As it was I contented myself with a brief glance within each apartment before I closed the door again.

I ate my dinner alone and was waited on by Astra who looked yellower and more dried-up than ever. My attempts to draw her into conversation were fruitless. She confined her answers to brief monosyllables and even my liveliest attempts at chatter evoked no response. I thought she seemed tired and tense, but when I asked her if the work she did was too hard she shook her head vehemently.

'I have worked very hard since I was a little child in Peking. Yang and I grew up in the

86

house of Madam Silver Moon's father. He was a most wealthy gentleman.'

'And my father, Eben Fletcher, came there?'

'Yes, Missy. Those were bad times, with the foreign men not allowed into our cities, and the barbarians sweeping down from the north, and the old master sick and close to death, and Madam Silver Moon was very happy to come here with the merchant, Eben Fletcher.'

'And you and Yang came, too.'

'Yang and I went everywhere with Madam Silver Moon. The master understood that. We were her body-servants,' Astra said with gentle dignity.

'You were fond of her?'

The question was futile, almost impertinent and I knew it as soon as I had spoken, for a blaze of adoration lit her face, her narrow eyes filled with tears, and she bowed deeply and wordlessly several times.

I swung round in my chair.

'My mother was killed. Madam Silver Moon was killed, Astra. And somebody means to kill me too,' I said earnestly.

'No, Missy! No harm will come to you. I tell you that you will be safe. Yang and I will protect you with our lives.'

'Yang and you are both old,' I said. 'You mean well, I know, but you cannot be with me every waking and sleeping moment for the next three weeks. After that, unless I make a new will, they will watch me as they watched

87

my father, waiting for me to die! Astra, if you know something you must tell me.'

I stopped, for into her face had come an expression that I can only describe as recognition. A recognition of something, or somebody, half-expected and wholly terrifying!

I turned and saw Uncle Daniel in the doorway behind me. He was still in cloak and riding boots, his heavy face flushed with exercise.

'My apologies. I meant to come home in time for dinner, but Mr. Fleetwood insisted that I stay. His good lady discovered that her family rubies have gone and she's been enjoying the vapours ever since. Now she won't be able to appear at parties wearing the only pigeon rubies in the district!'

As he spoke, he tossed his hat on to a chair and took his place at the table. His eyes raked Astra's face for a moment. 'You look as if you'd just lost five hundred pounds instead of gaining it. Get me something to eat, woman,' he said.

She bowed silently, and went out, pausing at the door to give him a fleeting glance in which fear and hatred were inextricably mingled.

'Queer woman,' Uncle Daniel remarked, pouring himself a drink. 'One can never tell what these foreigners are thinking!'

'If you'll excuse me, I have some letters to write,' I said, my voice steady though my hands were shaking.

88

'You're not afraid to sit at table with me, are you?' Uncle Daniel asked. 'I tell you that you've nothing to fear from me. I won't pretend I was pleased at the will. After all, I was Eben's only surviving brother and one might have expected more than a thousand, but I bear no grudges. No grudge in the world.'

He beamed at me, tossing back the last of his drink. I think I made some reply though I cannot now recall what it was. All that was in my mind at that instant was a desperate need to get out of the room, before I gave away the suspicions that crowded in on me.

I was not certain until I stood outside the door of Uncle Daniel's room what I intended to do, but my hand turned the knob before my brain began to instruct my nerves.

I closed the door softly behind me and gazed round the big, ornately decorated apartment in which the original wallpaper and pale hangings had been swamped by a number of sporting prints.

Now that I was here, I had no idea where to search. Indeed I had no idea what I was seeking. Evidence that he had killed my mother, I supposed, but surely if proof of his guilt existed he would have destroyed it eighteen years before. Only an idiot would keep such a thing. But what thing? I puzzled over this even while I hurried round, opening drawers and ruffling through the contents with nothing in my mind but a whirl of vague, unconnected fears and questions.

Uncle Daniel had been my father's heir until my father, having married Silver Moon, sired a daughter. Uncle Daniel had stayed on at Moonflete waiting patiently for Eben to die. No need for him to murder my father. I was sure that Daniel Fletcher was quite content to live at his brother's expense, waiting until all the property descended to him.

There was nothing here! Nothing! I swung round on my heel in disgust, searching for something I would probably not recognise if I found it. The toe of my slipper caught momentarily in a crack between two of the deep blue rugs covering the floor, I tugged my foot away impatiently and in so doing lost my balance for a split second, clutched at an open drawer to save myself and pulled it inadvertently to the ground.

The crash seemed to echo through the house, deafening me! I scrambled to my feet and waited for footsteps in the corridor, the thrusting open of the door, the outraged voice of the man to whom this bedroom had always belonged. There was nothing. In a house as large as this one the crash of a drawer would be no more than the toss of a pebble in the river.

My heart was knocking against the high-necked bodice of the dress I had chosen from the wardrobe, and there was perspiration on my forehead and the palms of my hands.

I began to stuff back the spilled articles into the drawer, rumpling cravats and handkerchiefs together in my frantic haste. There was nothing here to prove my suspicions or to explain that look of terrified recognition on old Astra's face. I knelt to pick up the drawer and slide it back into its groove.

The runners were loose and the drawer slipped in easily enough but caught suddenly on some projection within. I took out the drawer and bent to examine the obstruction. I could discern a faint glint at the back of the cabinet and I put in my hand to draw it out. It tore slightly as it came but it was quite easy to recognise what it had been.

It was a scarf of faded blue silk, its border heavily embossed with a design in seed pearls and gold thread of tiny half moons dangling from ropes of golden stars!

I held it in my hands, stretching the fine silk between my fingers. This was a lady's scarf, delicately exotic. I could imagine it flung over a small, proud Chinese head. It told me nothing that I had not already begun to guess, but my fear grew until it was a living, throbbing thing within me.

My teeth chattered and my hands shook as I bundled everything into the drawers, pushed them into place, straightened the carpets and rose with the scarf hanging limply from my fingers.

I would take the scarf to Astra, I decided. I

would ask her if she recognised it and beg her to suggest some reason, any reason, why it should be in Uncle Daniel's room. The thought that such a scarf might be looped about an unsuspecting neck, twisted and pulled tight, was an unpleasantly chilling one. I rolled up the soft, glinting stuff and pushed it again to the back of the drawer. Then I cautiously opened the door again and went out into the passage.

I could retrieve the scarf at some other time, I decided. First I must confirm my own fears by questioning Astra, by making her tell me about Uncle Daniel. But I must sponge my face and sit down for a few minutes until I could collect my senses. If anybody saw me now they would know at once that something terrible had happened. But nothing had happened! I had found an old scarf, that was all. A scarf that must have belonged to my mother but was now in a drawer full of my uncle's neckties and handkerchiefs.

My thoughts flitted to and fro, pecking at my brain like angry birds. In the hall below, as I stopped at the landing before the stained glass window, Astra was standing.

I could see the neat parting in her coiled white hair and her bent shoulders. As if drawn by my own gaze her eyes lifted to my face. I saw her lips move and then Uncle Daniel came out of the dining room.

'I promised Heather I'd look in on her this

afternoon. Stephen and Matthew will be in soon, and Frank promised to come over. We won't be long,' he called up to me.

'We?'

'Astra always goes to see Cherry on Tuesday afternoons when Cherry's staying at Jason Hall,' Uncle Daniel shouted up cheerfully.

'I want Astra to stay here,' I began to say, but my mouth was so dry that the words came out as an unintelligible croak.

Astra gave a jerky little bow and moved away, and Uncle Daniel followed her, lifting his hand in a casual salute.

For a moment I clung to the rail, the hall below tilting crazily as a wave of dizziness went over me. Then my vision cleared and I chided myself for foolishness.

He would take Astra to Jason Hall as was apparently her custom and bring her back when his own visit was finished. And she had made no protest but had gone willingly which meant I must have exaggerated that look of terror I had seen on her face.

Yang's quiet step below brought my heart jumping up into my throat again. My nerves, I thought, were becoming ragged. I came downstairs slowly to meet the old servant's smiling bow.

'Will Missy take a cup of lemon tea?' he asked gently. 'It is most refreshing at this time. Madam Silver Moon—'

'Always enjoyed a cup,' I said wearily.

'Missy?'

'It's nothing. I'm tired and a cup of lemon tea would be very nice,' I said quickly.

His face widened into a smile and he bowed again, tucking his hands into the wide sleeves of his short tunic.

'Does Astra always go on Tuesdays to see Miss Cherry?' I enquired.

'Oh yes, Missy. Always for many years. Madam Silver Moon allowed it.'

'Will Astra come home soon?'

'Oh yes, Missy. Astra always comes home before supper,' he assured me.

I smiled and went aimlessly into the garden room. It was hot in here with the perfume of forced flowers. Through the windows I could see a slender figure in black crossing the grass. Then Cherry raised her hand to me and hurried round to the door.

CHAPTER EIGHT

Her first words banished the suspicion that had gripped me. 'I thought that I'd come and visit Astra instead of having her come to Jason Hall,' she announced. 'And I wanted to see you too, Melody.'

'Astra just left with your father. I assume they took the gig,' I told her.

'I took the back road,' she said with an air of

annoyance. 'I would have met them otherwise on the path. Never mind, it was you I really wanted to see.'

'Yes, of course.'

I indicated a chair and sat down myself.

'I was wondering how soon we could go out of mourning,' she said frankly. 'I look hideous in black anyway, and you're not wearing it.'

'That's true,' I admitted. 'But you knew my father very closely for many years, and I would have thought—'

'That I was attached to him and very sorry for his death?' She shook her head. 'He was very kind, I suppose, but he wanted to own us all, to keep us all at Moonflete. He resented it when Heather and Frank stayed at Jason Hall. I think that he regretted having given the house back to her. And he didn't like it when I went over so often to stay.'

'Why did you?' I asked curiously. 'I don't get the impression that you're very fond of Heather and I know you dislike Frank.'

'They're toad-eaters,' she said, wrinkling her nose. 'When Heather's father died and Uncle Eben bought Jason Hall, Heather agreed to stay as housekeeper. And then Uncle Eben came back with his new wife and began to build Moonflete, and when Heather married he gave Jason Hall back to her and she took me there until I was old enough not to need a nurse. She agreed to every single thing that was arranged and she and Frank are forever ramming it down my throat how grateful they are to dear Uncle Eben for his generosity! But their company was preferable to living here, with my uncle wanting to know what I was doing at every moment of the day and my father telling me that I must be docile and sweet, because one day Moonflete would be mine!'

'And didn't you want it?' I asked.

Cherry shook her blonde head.

'I don't want to go on living here anyway,' she said frankly. 'I want to go down to London and move about in the best society, and make a wealthy marriage.'

'I gather Heather hoped you might marry Frank,' I hinted.

'So that Frank would be master of Moonflete one day. Well, I wouldn't have Frank on a plate, and he doesn't want me either. So the will stopped all of Heather's silly matchmaking plans.'

One of the maids came in then with two glasses of lemon tea and some wafer biscuits. As soon as she had gone, Cherry leaned forward.

'Would you mind very much if I put off my black dresses? I could wear grey or lilac,' she said earnestly.

'Wear scarlet if it pleases you,' I said flippantly.

It seemed so ridiculous to be solemnly discussing the impropriety of leaving off mourning with the daughter of the man whom I suspected of having killed my mother. Cherry's shallow good-natured mind seemed relieved however.

'I shall wear blue. It's my best colour and I always look pretty in it,' she said complacently. 'It almost seems a pity though, to waste it on the family.'

'Don't you like Matthew or Stephen either?'

Cherry shrugged and pouted.

'Stephen likes money,' she said. 'That's why he's stayed on all these years, hoping for a little bit of the property. He'd like to re-open the mill and sit all day counting the profits.'

'And Matthew?'

'Oh, he wants to open up the mill too, bring back the millhands, make Jason prosperous again.'

So each member of the family had a ruling passion, I thought. Cherry wanted to dazzle London society while her father saw her as the chatelain at Moonflete. Stephen liked money for its own sake, while Matthew had a dream of clipper ships and full employment. And Heather needed to winter abroad; and Frank—who knew Frank's ambitions?

'Cherry, it will take more than a thousand pounds to launch you properly into society,' I said impulsively. 'I wondered if you might care to accept—'

'Oh, are you going to offer me more? I hoped that you might be,' she exclaimed.

97

'You wouldn't be offended?'

'Heavens, no! Call it a loan if you like. Anything to get away from this place!'

She looked disparagingly round the flower-filled room, and immediately began to discuss the styles that best suited her.

I let her ramble on while in my own mind I turned over the significance of what I had found in Uncle Daniel's room. If I had guessed right and he had killed my mother then it would be only kind on my part to give Cherry the means to make a new life for herself in London.

'I'll walk back with you to Jason Hall,' I said abruptly, breaking into her chatter. 'Then Astra and I can come back together.'

'She usually comes down to see me on Tuesdays,' Cherry said, pulling up the hood of her cape. 'I think it started years ago when I was a baby and Astra used to take care of me sometimes. She's such a creature of habit that she's gone on doing it ever since.'

'I'm surprised the two of them didn't go back to China, after my mother had died,' I said, taking my own mantle for the afternoon had turned cool.

'Why should they?' Cherry asked. 'I suppose they hoped for a long time that Silver Moon might return. And then they thought Uncle Eben was the greatest man on earth. Everything he ever did was quite perfect in their eyes, simply because he'd married their beloved "Madam".'

I walked as briskly as I could without leaving the sauntering Cherry behind. It was a pleasantly sharp afternoon in the breeze and the moors rolling away on every side seemed limitless.

A mounted figure on the horizon changed course and galloped towards us. It was Matthew, and the customary scowl drew his brows together which made my own involuntary smile seem unreasoned, as foolish as Cherry's chatter.

'I've been making enquiries about the robbery last night,' he said, reining in his mount, and staring down at us.

'Have you found out anything?' I asked.

'The pattern's the same as before. Two sets of lights flashing—they always seem to come at irregular intervals from a different part of the valley. Horses heard galloping across the moor, and then this morning some unfortunate householder finds his wife's rubies gone. A side door had been forced; somebody *thinks* they heard the dogs barking; nobody has seen a thing.'

'Were there no tracks?' I asked.

'Over the other side of the valley there were the tracks of five or six horses going towards Rochdale. At Fleetwood Hall there were no tracks within a mile of the house. What do you make of that, young ladies?'

'That the horses were a decoy,' I said. 'Were

99

they seen last night?'

Matthew shook his head. 'Only heard. And one or two people noticed the lights flashing. They were nowhere in the vicinity of Fleetwood Hall either.'

'So that everybody at that side of the valley went happily to bed, congratulating themselves on their good fortune,' I said.

'Decoys. Exactly!' He nodded approvingly. 'This is the fifth robbery in the past twelve months, and each time the robbery has taken place in the opposite direction from where the lights were seen and the horses heard.'

'So while everybody in one area bolts their door and hides their heads under the blankets, somebody walks up to another house and calmly robs it.'

'Taking away only what can be carried on his person,' Matthew finished. 'The Fleetwood rubies, the Astley silver cups, some gold coins that had been in Colonel Ayre's family for generations.'

'And nothing from Moonflete,' I said slowly. 'What about Jason Hall?'

'There's nothing at Jason Hall worth the taking,' Cherry put in. 'It doesn't stop Heather from double-bolting every door, however.'

'I'm on my way back from Heather now. She was expecting Uncle Daniel to call in and keep her up-to-date with the news,' Matthew began.

'But Uncle Daniel went over to Jason Hall some time ago,' I said in alarm. 'He took Astra

100

with him.'

'Neither he nor Astra were at the hall,' Matthew frowned. 'Perhaps he changed his mind.'

'He said he was going to see Heather, and Astra went with him,' I persisted.

'Then he stopped off somewhere,' Matthew said. 'There's no need to look so stricken, Melody. My uncle isn't the most reliable person in the world.'

I bit my lip, longing to cry out, 'Your uncle is worse than unreliable. He has a scarf belonging to my mother in his bedroom drawer and Astra is afraid when she looks at him.'

Aloud I said, 'Cherry and I are going down to Jason Hall now. We'll see if Uncle Daniel and Astra have arrived yet.'

I set off again at a faster step than before, with Cherry bestirring herself to keep pace. I daresay that Matthew thought it grossly impolite of me to hurry away without any word of farewell, but at that moment I was concerned only with the finding of Astra. I couldn't forget the look I had seen on her face nor the droop of her shoulders as if she carried some knowledge or burden too great to be endured.

The gates of Jason Hall were open, the drive curving between the trees to the grey stone facade of the house. There was no sign of the gig.

Cherry took the key from her reticule and opened the front door, letting us into a square, high-ceilinged hall with a couple of mouldering stags' heads on brown walls disfigured by patches of damp.

'It's falling to pieces,' Cherry said carelessly. 'Neither Heather nor Frank has the money to run it properly.'

She lifted her voice and called up into the emptiness.

'Heather! Heather! Are you there?'

'I'm in here, Cherry.'

Heather's voice sounded through a door at the back of the hall.

Cherry rustled ahead of me, opening the door into a square-panelled room where patched rugs and a small fire spoke of genteel poverty.

'I never expected you back so soon, my dear,' Heather began, rising from a chair by the side of the hearth. She stopped short at seeing me, and raised her eyebrows faintly as if my presence were an intrusion.

'Melody is going to give me a lot of money so that I can go to London,' Cherry said. 'And we don't need to wear mourning any longer.'

'I will wear black out of respect for Eben's memory for the customary three years,' Heather said stiffly.

'We came over to see if Uncle Daniel and Astra were here,' I broke in.

'I've been waiting here since dinner time,'

Heather said, resuming her seat with an annoyed air. 'Daniel promised to look in and tell me about the robbery at Fleetwood Hall. And Frank rode off to meet Stephen this morning and won't be back until dinner. Meanwhile anybody could break in here, though it's hardly worth their while.'

She looked disparagingly about the shabby apartment.

'There's no need for you to stay here,' I said, speaking almost without thought as I tried frantically to imagine where Uncle Daniel and Astra could possibly be. 'You and Cherry ought to come back to Moonflete as chaperones if nothing else.'

'Chaperones!' Cherry giggled, her hand to her mouth. 'Heavens, nobody bothers very much about chaperones round here.'

'It's difficult to realise that you're only eighteen,' Heather said. 'You seem older. No doubt it's because of that cool, quiet manner. Silver Moon had it, too. One never knew what she was thinking.'

'Here's father,' Cherry exclaimed, glancing through a side window.

'Is Astra with him?' I demanded.

'No. He's by himself. I'll let him in.'

Cherry went out into the hall again.

Heather looked up at me and said with a visible effort, 'You're being very kind, I know. Your father was kind, too. If you wish us to come back to Moonflete for a little while, we'll come. But you must make some more permanent arrangement as soon as it can be managed. *This* is my home.'

'Father says that he left Astra at the gates and drove down into the village,' Cherry said, coming back.

Behind her, Uncle Daniel loomed, big and genial, with something uneasy in his smile.

'Shaft on the gig was loose. I took it into Benson to get it tightened. He kept me talking about the robbery and then I came back here,' Uncle Daniel said.

Astra hasn't come,' Heather said,

'I decided to walk up to Moonflete to see Astra there but Melody said that I'd just missed you,' Cherry put in.

'Well, she probably saw one of the servants, heard Cherry had gone up to Moonflete and decided to walk back,' her father said.

'It's Mary's afternoon off, and Cook is indulging in a migraine because the fish didn't arrive,' Heather said. Her tone implied that the occupants of Jason Hall couldn't afford to employ more than two servants.

'She'll be back at Moonflete, I daresay. No need to fuss because an old woman takes it into her head to turn back,' Uncle Daniel persisted.

'Heather and Cherry are coming back to Moonflete with me for a while,' I told him.

'Just as well, with these robberies going on,' he agreed. 'I had a walk round the house just

104

now and your doors and windows seem well-guarded, but one can't be too careful. Better for us all to be together!'

'I'm going back now. Cherry and Heather can follow,' I said.

It was imperative that I find Astra. Imperative that I get back to Moonflete and take that scarf from Uncle Daniel's room again. I had been a complete fool to put it back in the first place, but events were crowding in on me. I was surrounded by people whose lips spoke one thing while their eyes said something else. And I was letting myself be used and manipulated as my father had used and manipulated me.

'Shall I drive you back?' Uncle Daniel said, but I shook my head, muttering something about their needing the gig for Heather's and Cherry's luggage, and hurried through the shabby hall.

Outside the house I paused for an instant, drawn by some compulsion impossible to resist to the side of the house. Uncle Daniel had come from the back of the house, having checked the locks, or so he said.

I walked on the grass verge, behind the fringe of trees that would shield me from the side window, and gained the overgrown garden, ragged with bindweed and bushes.

The windows at the back were shuttered and bolted, blank eyes in a grey face. Behind me stood a row of sheds with broken eaves and doors teetering on their hinges.

Obviously there was nothing in the out-buildings that needed locking away. Nothing, I told myself firmly, even as I went to the first door and looked in at a pile of kindling and a row of cobwebbed tools. There was nothing in the second shed either except a pile of coal. Nothing in the third except old sacks thrown hither and thither in the gloom of a windowless interior.

If anybody found me poking about here they would be quite justified in thinking me neurotic, I decided, but I went into the shed, stepping over the broken flagstones, bending down to the pile of sacks and then turning slowly, caught by a gleam of colour in the corner.

It was Astra's blue shawl and Astra herself sat neatly with her feet together, her shawled head bowed over her knees. A kitchen knife, long-bladed and sharp, protruded from her stomach and her hands were clenched in death about the handle.

Astra was quite dead! The sentence formed itself quite coldly in my numbed brain. Uncle Daniel *must* have killed her. In the gig, driving home the knife secreted in his sleeve, carrying her to the back of the house. But I must find definite proof. The old servant could only have suspected, but she must have revealed her suspicions too clearly and now she was dead.

I leaned against the wall for a moment,

fighting back nausea. Then I straightened up and went back down the side path through the gates, and up the road towards Moonflete.

I walked slowly but in my mind a plan was forming as fast as I could think.

CHAPTER NINE

When I reached Moonflete I went upstairs and let myself again into Uncle Daniel's room. The blue scarf with its border of pearls and gold was still in the drawer where I had hastily pushed it. I retrieved it from its hiding place and took it back to my own room where I put it in the dragon-painted cabinet with the moonstones.

Moonstones! Running them through my fingers I realised I had forgotten the moonstones. Yet that was how it had all begun—with the parcel left on the bird tray in my London home. Somebody had left it there, whether as gift or warning I couldn't tell. But *somebody* had known where I lived. The necklace had frightened Astra. It had terrified her on my first evening here and she had begged me not to show it to anybody.

I turned the silver chain over and over, examining each link, each stone, but it was a perfectly ordinary trinket. Well, not precisely ordinary, I thought. The workmanship was exquisite, the settings obviously old and rare, but there was nothing here to cause an old servant to display such fear.

I changed unaided into one of Silver Moon's prettiest outfits, a tunic of soft yellow silk, with narrow trousers embroidered down the sides with jet beads. Then I hung the moonstones around my neck where they lay like a collar above the yellow silk. I brushed my hair and coiled it in loops over my ears.

The face that looked back at me from the mirror was strained, eyes dark-shadowed, skin drawn tightly over ivory-tinted cheekbones. I pinched colour into my lips and applied some glittery stuff from one of the pots on the dressing-table to my eyelids. My hands were quite steady now.

Gloomy clouds were racing across the sky, heralding a stormy evening, but there were still streaks of sunlit blue. The fire in my room had not been lit, presumably because this was Astra's usual task, and the white walls and hangings struck a chill into me.

I took a furred cloak from the wardrobe and slipped it around my shoulders. It was better to assuage my nervousness with a short walk than with a fruitless wait in apartments that seemed now alien to me despite their beauty.

I let myself through the bathroom door and went down the outside stair into the little enclosed yard which contained the well from which our water was drawn up. The kitchen door opened into the yard and I went through the big, flag-stoned room with its glowing range into the short passage which led to the outer yard.

As I passed the scullery door, Yang came out with a jar of damsons in his hands, and an anxious expression on his face.

'If you please, Missy, will Astra soon be back?' he enquired after the usual bow.

I said nothing but stared at him stupidly, my mind filled with the memory of Astra as I had seen her, hunched over the knife.

'Miss Cherry is here now with Madam Heather,' the old man went on. 'But they tell me that Astra did not go into Jason Hall. It is now necessary for me to do her share of the work also. Astra did not tell you where she intended to go?'

'She said nothing,' I answered truthfully.

Yang shook his head.

'That Astra grows stupid with age,' he said. 'Since you came, Missy, she has been most troubled in her mind, but to me she says nothing.'

'Nor to me,' I said.

The temptation to confide in Yang, if only to save him hours of uncertainty, was strong in me. But Yang was old and it might be safer for him to know nothing.

I went on through the side door into the stableyard. The gig was there and the red-faced coachman was taking out a pile of bandboxes. Evidently Heather and Cherry, having to return, had planned upon a long stay. I accepted the man's nod.

It had crossed my mind that I might tell the servants about the terms of the will but I had dismissed the idea. Apart from the two Chinese servants, none of the household staff had been at Moonflete for more than ten years, and none of them were local folk. If they gossiped about the sudden arrival of a daughter they did it where I couldn't hear.

It would be unfair to involve them in any possible danger to me, and the shrewd, practical part of my nature warned me, moreover, that if I made it known that I was aware of a murderer in the family, I might find myself with no servants at all, except old Yang.

I had traversed the stable yard and was walking down the steep path up which Yang had driven me in the shabby little carriage. On either side of me the grass dipped and rose starred with pale sprigs of early heather and meadowsweet. Overhead a crow soared, its raucous voice unpleasant above the sighing wind.

So much had happened since I came to Moonflete, I thought. In walking through the door into that white bedroom, I had closed the door of my former life behind me. I had found myself in a circle of people whom I could not trust, involved in a story that had begun before I was born and would end—with my death? I shivered, pulling the heavy cloak further around me.

From nearby came a ripple of laughter. I started, having believed myself alone, but a few steps brought me up to the rim of a grassy hollow which ringed round a pool fed by a little stream that wandered down between ferns bent back from the wind.

Cherry, still in her black dress, was throwing pebbles into the water and laughing as she did so, with her hood thrown back, and her blonde ringlets trailing over her slender neck. Her companion, in riding clothes with greenish gilt hair uncovered, was Matthew. His shoulders were also shaking with mirth as I approached them.

'Oh Lord! I hope I am about when that happens. It will be a marvellous sight to see,' he said.

I was completely unprepared for the tempest of feeling that swept over me, flooding me full of such jealousy that even fear was momentarily driven out. Jealousy of the rosy-cheeked blonde who laughed up into Matthew's sullen face. But he was smiling now, his face warm, his voice deeply pleasant. I had not caused him to smile, let alone laugh since I came to Moonflete. And I knew suddenly that I wanted, above all things, to bring laughter into Matthew Fletcher's face.

The smile died on his lips as he looked up and saw me. Then Cherry turned, still laughing.

Ah, Melody!' she called out. 'I was telling Matthew that when I go to London I intend to catch a Duke at least. Matthew says he would like to see that!'

'I thought you were in the house,' I said, my voice sharper than I had intended.

'I came out for a breath of air. Heather is busily complaining to father about the way I talk to her precious Frank,' Cherry said. 'Matthew was on his way home.'

'You don't have to explain all your movements to me,' I said as lightly as I could.

'I'm so used to having to explain all my movements to Uncle Eben,' Cherry pouted. 'I was telling Matthew about Astra.'

'Astra?' my voice squeaked.

'About her not arriving at Jason Hall,' Cherry said, with a slightly surprised air at my manner. 'Yang told Heather and me that she hadn't come back to Moonflete, either. Wouldn't it be odd if she never came back at all!'

'That's a stupid way to talk,' Matthew said shortly.

'Because Melody might be frightened? You don't really feel afraid, do you?' Cherry enquired.

'Of course she feels afraid!' Matthew swung round on her impatiently. 'Good God, Cherry, are you completely without imagination! Melody knows very well that her mother was killed. She knows that each one of us has a financial motive for murdering her within three weeks. Of course she's afraid! That's why she tried to buy you off by promising to launch you in London.'

'That's a lie!' I exclaimed. 'Cherry, it's not true. Matthew won't give me any credit for disinterested kindness. But it's not true. I simply wanted to be generous. Is there any reason why I shouldn't be generous?'

'Why should you?' he retorted. 'Your mother never was!'

The sentence hit me like a blow between the eyes. I pressed my lips together and clenched my fists, willing back the words that sprang up in me. When I did speak I made my voice as toneless as possible.

'Cherry, would you do me the favour of going back to the house? I would like a private word with my cousin.'

Something in my face must have belied my voice, for Cherry stepped back, gave a nervous little giggle and then, picking up her full skirts, hurried away.

When I looked again at Matthew, the flash of feeling had vanished from his expression and he met me with his customary brooding look.

'Are you going to offer *me* money to launch myself into society?' he enquired. 'Or did you hope I might be induced to accept a little something on account towards the opening up

113

of the mill?'

'I wouldn't give you any of my money if you got down on your knees and begged for it!' I cried furiously. 'I don't care if you do kill me for it. You'd be found out and hanged!'

'I've no intention of killing you, and no intention of begging for money either,' Matthew said coldly.

His coldness served to inflame my own temper and I ranted on, aware dimly that I erected my rage as a barrier against my fear and the horror of that seated figure in the shed at Jason Hall.

'And no intention of treating me with the slightest kindness or concern either!' I shrilled. 'You must have hated my mother! You really must have hated her.'

'She was very beautiful,' he said.

'And ungenerous! That was what you said, wasn't it? Ungenerous! Why? What did my mother refuse you, Matthew? What did she refuse?'

My words were stifled against a hard, demanding mouth and my hands were tugged at thick, green-gilt hair, and then relaxing into the tresses as all desire to thrust him away melted in the flames of a greater desire, to hold him so closely that our hearts and bodies would merge.

Then he pulled down my hands and held them bruisingly between his own hard palms, and his eyes were cold with an ice that burned through me hotter than fire.

'She refused me *that*!' he said. 'Silver Moon refused me *that*!'

And he flung away my hands and rubbed the corner of his cloak across his lips as if to wipe away the touch of my mouth.

'You were sixteen,' I whispered.

'Sixteen,' he agreed. 'Do you know what it's like to be sixteen? Do you know what it's like to have all the instincts of a healthy young animal? To be crammed so full of life that you feel one sweep of your arms could blow mountains away! To be so full of love that every girl you pass in the course of a day becomes for an instant a symbol of all that is womanly!'

'Silver Moon was my mother—your uncle's bride!'

'She was eighteen, so small and delicate that I could have broken her between my two hands,' Matthew said on a groan. 'She could speak a little English, not much but enough to make conversation with her a joy. She was young, and my uncle was old. Past fifty and set in his ways. A hard, ungenerous man who had collected a beautiful wife in the same way that he amassed his treasures for the building of Moonflete.'

'And you loved Silver Moon?'

'I hated her,' said Matthew. 'I hated her for being so lovely, so cool, so out-of-reach. She never showed me one spark of true kindness.

115

There was none in her.'

'You said she was ungenerous.'

'For two years, first at Jason Hall and then at Moonflete I saw her every day,' Matthew said. 'I used to watch her, sitting at table and smiling, in her beautiful clothes with her tiny, bound feet. She knew that I watched her. I think she found it amusing. To make herself so lovely that a boy couldn't drag his eyes away. I loathed what she was doing but she made all other women seem insipid to me.'

I faced him in the dying sunlight close to the little rippling pool and asked the question that I had to ask, though I feared the answer.

'What happened on the night she disappeared? What really happened?'

'She'd been out of sorts for a day or two,' he said slowly. 'I think she was bored with everything. I came home early from the mill to see if the rotting trees in the copse had been felled. At least that was the reason I gave to myself. I knew deep down that I wanted to see Silver Moon, to see her in the way one probes a sore tooth with one's tongue, unable to resist the pain. She was in her room but the door was open and she called to me, inviting me in. We talked for a little while. She was *very* sweet. Silver Moon could be very sweet.'

'And then?' I prompted.

'She began to compliment me,' he said. 'She compared me with Uncle Eben. He was old, she said, and since the birth of her child he'd lost interest in her. And I was young and strong. She made it all so convincing.'

'And you tried to kiss her?'

'I was fool enough to ask,' he said bitterly. 'I told her how lovely she was and how I suffered to see her every day and be unable to say anything of my desires. I actually sat there like an idiot, telling her all this. And she listened with that small curve of the lips as if she were tasting cream. I can see her now—in a long robe of soft white stuff with a blue scarf about her shoulders. There was a border of pearls and little gold stars on the scarf, and all the time I was talking she kept drawing her long fingernails across the design with a little rasping sound.'

I was as still as the pebbles that lay about the edge of the pool, my eyes fixed on his face.

'And then she laughed,' said Matthew. 'She laughed and told me how silly I was to imagine she could feel anything for a young barbarian, who worked with his hands for no payment, like a slave. She sat there laughing, with her eyes glinting and her hands stroking the scarf.'

He fell silent, his eyes gazing at the past. When he resumed, his voice was flatly matter-of-fact, as if he were tired of the recital.

'I got up and flung out of the room, out of the house. I think I had some crazy notion of killing myself, but at eighteen one doesn't throw one's life away so easily. I spent the evening in one public house after another. It was late when I got back. I wasn't drunk. I hadn't even managed that. I went up to bed and in the morning I went down to the mill. The rest you know.'

'And you stayed on here, even after the mill was closed?'

'I wanted the money,' he said wryly. 'I thought it very likely that Uncle Eben would leave me a good portion of his property. It would have compensated me for something—lost innocence, I suppose. I know I swore never to love another woman, and never to ask before I took what I desired.'

'So you kissed me as a kind of belated revenge,' I said, and my heart was a small stone within me.

'I don't know why I kissed you,' he said moodily. 'To punish you for being your mother's child, I suppose.'

I knew then that I had to show myself different from my mother. And I could do it only by trusting myself to him with a generosity of spirit that Silver Moon had never shown.

'I know where Astra is,' I said, quickly and breathlessly before I could change my mind. 'She is in one of the sheds at the back of Jason Hall. Stabbed. I saw her there. She's dead and I'm the only one who knows, apart from the person who put her there.'

He gave me a long considering look as if he were weighing the value of my words. Then he turned away from me, his face shadowed.

When he looked at me again I could see a medley of conflicting emotions struggling for mastery in his face.

'You are the first person I've told,' I said again. 'Nobody else knows I've seen her.'

'I have to go to Jason Hall,' he said at last. 'I'll come back to Moonflete as soon as I can.'

He was gone then, striding over the grass to where his horse grazed nearby. I had made my gesture and could only hope that he had recognised and accepted it. Now there was nothing left but to return to Moonflete, with the moonstones round my neck and the faded blue scarf knotted about my shoulder, and wait for the terror in someone's eyes to give me the name of my mother's killer.

CHAPTER TEN

When I arrived back at the house, the candles and fires had been lit and a rosy glow within competed with the sunset outside. Yang was busy in the dining room, laying out plates with a great clattering as if to express his annoyance.

I hurried up to my own room and covered the moonstone necklace and the scarf with a short velvet cape. My hair had been ruffled slightly by the wind and there was no longer any need for me to bite colour into my lips.

The face that stared back at me in the mirror sparkled as if its owner had just come alive again. Yet danger was all around, a tragedy had occurred that same afternoon, and I had received a kiss meant for my mother.

When I went into the garden room, Uncle Daniel greeted me cheerfully, with a comment on my flushed cheeks, as he offered me a glass of sherry.

'Though I'm not certain if a young lady of eighteen should indulge in such intoxicants,' he teased pompously.

Privately I felt that a stiff brandy might be of more comfort to me than the sherry at that moment, but I accepted the glass and sat down a little apart from the others.

'No sign of Astra?' Heather asked.

She was ensconced in her chair with the inevitable knitting in her hands as if she had never spent a night away. And why, I wondered, had she gone back to Jason Hall in the first place?

I had spoken aloud, for she looked at me in surprise.

'Silver Moon would have wished me to go back to my own house.'

'Silver Moon was your friend. Wouldn't you have been welcome for a time in the home of your friend?' I asked.

A dull red ran up her neck into her sallow cheeks and she knitted more rapidly.

After a moment or two, she said in a low

voice, 'You are very kind, Melody. Eben was always very kind.'

'He was a selfish old skinflint,' Stephen said. 'No, Heather, I won't be quiet! It's time you woke up to the fact that Eben Fletcher was a mean, grasping man who thoroughly enjoyed turning you out of your home and then graciously handing it back to you when he'd denuded it of valuables. I'm sorry, Melody, but it has to be said. And it should be obvious to us all by now after hearing that infamous will that he was a man without the least regard for his daughter's safety!'

'But none of us would really kill Melody,' Cherry said.

She had changed into a pink dress sprigged with lilac and grey, and looked demurely charming as she sat sipping her drink.

'It's all very well for you to talk,' Stephen said. 'You're off to London in a month or two, to dazzle the dukes. What is there for me to do except find a post somewhere as a chartered accountant?'

'But Melody will give you what you need to start up somewhere on your own,' Cherry persisted.

'Thank you, but there's a slight difference between taking money from one's uncle and money from one's female cousin,' Stephen said.

'You've lived very well at Eben's expense all these years,' Heather said in a trembling voice.

'Isn't it a little late to begin developing moral scruples now?'

'I haven't noticed your precious son going short of anything,' Stephen drawled.

Heather's swollen knuckles tightened on the needles.

'Whoa there, now!' Uncle Daniel said placatingly. 'No call to talk to a lady like that!'

I had a sudden crazy desire to jump up and shout, 'While you squabble and bicker and tell your petty little lies, Astra is stiffening into cold flesh at the back of Jason Hall!' But I sat quietly, sipping my drink as daintily as Cherry was doing, and said nothing.

We were interrupted by Frank who hurried in, wind-blown and flushed, to pause by the steps, survey us gravely, and then enquire with great cordiality, 'Quarrelling again?'

'None of your damned cheek!' Uncle Daniel growled. 'You're late anyway. We're ready to go in to supper.'

'I arrived at Jason Hall expecting to be given supper there and was told by a decidedly bad-tempered cook that you and Cherry had come back here. Are you going to kill the fatted calf or something, Melody?'

'If you will excuse me, Missy.' Yang was bowing respectfully in the doorway.

'Yes, what is it?' I asked.

'Supper will be a little delayed, Missy. I have taken the liberty of asking some of the other servants to search for Astra.' His voice was tinged with reproach. Evidently he considered it remiss of me not to have instituted a search myself.

'It is odd that she's not here,' Cherry said with a puzzled air. 'And Matthew isn't back either.'

'Matthew's unpunctuality doesn't bother me in the least,' Heather said testily, winding her wool into a ball and sticking the needles through it vindictively. 'Don't you recall when we all went down to London in January how he was forever wandering off by himself?'

'You all went to London? In January?' My voice was strange in my own ears.

'Yes, dear.' She sounded impatient as if she were talking to a slow-witted child.

And that, I thought, was exactly how I had been behaving! The moonstone necklace had been left in the garden of my London house. Obviously, only somebody who had been in London during the month in which my birthday fell could have left the necklace there. That was the first thing I should have tried to find out!

'Why did you all go down to London?' I asked.

'Eben went down to consult a heart specialist,' Heather said. 'Daniel went with him and so did Matthew and Stephen.'

'We meant to make a bachelor holiday of it,' Stephen said with a grin, 'but when Heather heard of the trip she demanded to be allowed to go too.'

'I needed to consult a specialist myself,' she said haughtily. 'And I was right to do so. The specialist informed me that another winter in a northern climate might very well leave me a hopeless cripple.'

'So my mother went down to London too, and I trailed along for the ride,' said Frank.

'I was going to go,' said Cherry. 'I was looking forward to it so much but at the last moment Uncle Eben decided that I shouldn't be allowed to go. At the very last moment when all my boxes and trunks were packed, Uncle Eben decided that one of us had to remain behind.'

Her tone was deeply resentful.

Uncle Daniel said, with a spurious air of apology, 'I'd have stayed here with you, Cherry darling, but there seemed very little reason why I should—'

'Give up a free visit to London? No, of course not, why should you?' Cherry said bitterly.

So all of them except Cherry had been in London during January, I thought, and one of them must have put that moonstone necklace in the garden. But only my father had known I was still alive and had been aware of my address. For some reason my father must have left the necklace for me and then, later, as he lay dying he had muttered over and over, 'Moonstones! Moonstones!'

Under cover of the cloak I surreptitiously put my hand up to the gleaming collar at the neck of my tunic. I wished Matthew would hurry back. I needed someone by my side whom I could trust. Someone I could trust! I looked from Stephen's indolent face to Cherry's sulky one, to the needles clenched in Heather's hands, and the glass in Uncle Daniel's thick fingers. In the background Frank leaned, obviously savouring the argument. One of them had killed my mother. One of them might be planning to kill me. And I was no longer quite so certain about Uncle Daniel's guilt. He had certainly had a great deal to gain from my mother's death, I thought. But he had had even more to gain from my death. Why then had Silver Moon alone vanished? There was no point in killing the wife if the child was spared, which meant that some motive other than gain had inspired the guilty one. Unless, of course, Uncle Daniel had been interrupted in his task. Yet he had had time in which to hide away the blue scarf in his drawer—if it was Uncle Daniel who had hidden it there in the first place!

'Do we *have* to wait for Matthew before we eat?' Stephen demanded.

'Of course not. We'll go in now.'

I rose and led the way to the dining room. Supper was the last thing that interested me at this moment, but it was no longer possible to sit, pretending a calm I did not feel.

'Is Mr. Matthew not to eat?' Yang enquired as we took our places.

'He'll be here soon,' I began.

'Perhaps he decided to go off and look for Astra,' Cherry chimed in. 'Did he say where he was going when you were together?'

'Together? What were Matthew and Melody doing together?' Heather wanted to know.

'They were out on the moor talking,' Cherry began. 'Or rather, I was out there with Matthew, and Melody joined us. They wanted to talk privately so I came back to the house.'

'For someone whose death would be an advantage in certain quarters you do show yourself to be remarkably trusting,' Frank said to me gaily.

'I don't think that anyone will murder me,' I said, more confidently than I felt.

'Well, somebody killed her mother,' Cherry pointed out. 'And hid the body too, for it was never found.'

She put her hand over her wine glass to prevent Yang from refilling it and gazed round at us all, wide-eyed.

'I can't quite see Matthew as a suspect,' Uncle Daniel said, as casually as if we were discussing the theft of a napkin ring. 'Of course he has a violent side to his nature; has had ever since he was a boy. But he has a great respect for human life. He gets it from his father, I suppose. You'd have liked my brother

126

Tom. He was the best of the three of us.'

He beamed at me, having reached the stage when a man is not yet drunk, but no longer sober.

'Talking of moonstones—' I began.

'Were we? I didn't realise!'

'Talking of moonstones,' I repeated, and began to unfasten the short yellow cape, 'I forgot to tell you that I was given some particularly fine ones for my last birthday.'

The cape was loose now and I let it slide down to the back of my chair, while they stared at me, their eyes caught by moonstones gleaming at my neck.

'What a sweet necklace,' Cherry said admiringly.

'It was a gift,' I said again.

'But who gave it to you?' she asked.

'I found the scarf,' I said. 'It belonged to my mother, I think.'

Uncle Daniel's eyes were fixed upon it. Alert, sober eyes, bright with apprehension. He had certainly been shocked out of his half-drunken geniality.

'It's pretty, isn't it?' I said. 'The edge of it was caught in the drawer and it tore a little. Perhaps Astra will be able to mend it when she comes back.'

Uncle Daniel's fork rattled against the side of his plate. His normally florid hue had paled to a sickly white.

'I'd never dare to attempt it myself,'

127

Heather said. 'The work is too dainty for my hands. Knitting is all that I can manage.'

Yang was serving the dessert now, a preserve of damsons with thick yellow cream. Frank was teasing Cherry that it would spoil her figure and she was answering sharply that she cared nothing for his opinion. Uncle Daniel was still staring at me, as if he were hypnotised by my bright necklace and fluttering scarf.

I looked down at my plate and felt a sudden distaste for the meal. I could not have told what I had eaten, or indeed if I had eaten anything. I should have waited until Matthew arrived before I revealed the scarf and the necklace, for though Uncle Daniel was the picture of guilt there still seemed no way to bring it home to him. No way until Matthew came back as witness to Astra's death.

And Matthew should have been back by now. It would have taken him only a few minutes to ride down to Jason Hall. Even if he had sent for a local magistrate there wouldn't have been this delay.

I rose abruptly, pushing away my untasted dessert, and causing Frank to break off in the middle of a sentence. 'If you'll excuse me, I have a headache,' I said, my knuckles gleaming ivory yellow on the edge of the white cloth.

I couldn't stop looking at Uncle Daniel's sagging face and unhappy, frightened eyes. He had not risen as I left my chair but slumped at his place as if I had just delivered a judgement on him. Now I was certain in my own mind that he was guilty for he had the knowledge written all over his face. If only Matthew would return!

I went back to the garden room, ignoring the flurry of chatter between Heather and Cherry and the scraping of chairs as Stephen and Frank got hastily to their feet. In here the scent of flowers was overpowering, the fires banked up high to maintain an even temperature. The perfume was too sweet, drowning my senses. I turned back into the corridor, pushing past the others with some flustered, incoherent excuse, and re-entered the dining room.

Yang pulled at my sleeve as I entered, the unusually familiar gesture a sign of his perturbation.

'Please, Missy, Astra is not yet come and it grows dark,' he said.

'Not now, Yang. I'll see to it later,' I said, impatiently jerking my sleeve away.

'I beg Missy's pardon.'

He bowed and went softly away.

At the table Uncle Daniel was still slumped, staring unseeingly before him. I went and stood before him with only the width of the table between us.

'Matthew will be back soon,' I said harshly.

'You found that blue scarf in my room,' Uncle Daniel said, without changing the direction of his gaze. 'You went into my room and found it.'

'You were the one,' I said, slowly and shakily. 'It was you.'

Uncle Daniel nodded and reached for the decanter, as if even in that moment of revelation he clung to his small vices.

'It was. Eben suspected it but never could be certain,' he said thickly. 'I was a fool to keep the scarf. It was at the back of the drawer and I thought it was safe enough, but I should have destroyed it long ago. Long ago.'

'Astra knew. Astra guessed,' I whispered.

'She told me so, on the way to Jason Hall,' he agreed.

'Matthew will be here soon,' I said stupidly.

'But you won't tell him,' said Uncle Daniel.

It was not a question but a statement and his eyes glittered at me suddenly.

'I'll tell the others. I have only to call,' I said, my lips dry.

'They won't believe you,' said Uncle Daniel. 'You're the stranger here, like Silver Moon, and they won't believe you.'

'There's the scarf, and the moonstones.'

'You found an old scarf, and I know nothing of moonstones,' he said. 'They won't believe you, Melody. There's no proof now.'

'I'll get Matthew,' I burst out, and fear swelled into panic as Uncle Daniel rose heavily, still clutching the decanter.

I turned and ran as fast as I possibly could

out of the door into the long corridor which twisted towards the great entrance hall. Behind me I heard Uncle Daniel shout but I tugged open the door and ran out on to the gravel path.

Before me the road dipped down to Jason Hall and the village beyond. I hesitated for an instant and then the thickset figure of Uncle Daniel loomed up on the threshold of the candle-lit hall.

I ran wildly then, swerving down the path, hearing with the greatest relief the thudding of approaching hooves.

'Matthew! Matthew!'

My voice rose, thin and frightened in the wind.

The horse slowed to a trot and shivered to a halt as my hands reached out to grasp the bridle. The horse was riderless, the saddle empty and as I brought my hand away I felt and smelled the warm saltiness of fresh blood.

CHAPTER ELEVEN

The horse jerked away from my restraining fingers and continued its homeward trot. I heard another shout from the door but the wind caught the sound, whirling it away, and then I was running again down the path, running freely without the constriction of whalebone stays and hampering skirts, with the thin silk trousers rippling like water against my legs.

Jason Hall was in darkness save for a faint glimmering of light in the kitchen windows. I assumed the cook had recovered from her migraine and Mary had come back from her afternoon out; no doubt they would be enjoying a pot of tea and a gossip about Heather's return to Moonflete.

I made my way round to the back of the house and called softly.

'Matthew! Matthew!'

There was no answer save the rustling of leaves overhead and the sighing of wind across the yard.

I hesitated, looking back over my shoulder for fear I had been pursued, but nothing loomed out of the darkness there. I went cautiously forward again, placing my flat-heeled slippers carefully on the uneven flag-stones.

Opposite, beneath a thin sliver of moon, yawned the broken doors of the sheds. I paused, held back by my own nervousness, yet knowing that I ought to look inside those sheds; but the terrible fear that two bodies, instead of one, sat silently within paralysed my will.

'Matthew!' I called again, 'Please answer me!'

But still no answer came, and I forced

myself to move forward again, across the yard towards those open sheds.

There was no light at all inside the low-roofed windowless stone buildings. I stood still, accustoming my eyes to the density of darkness. Gradually objects assumed shape and form—the rusting tools, the sacks.

I turned towards the corner, forcing my reluctant eyes to gaze again at that huddled figure. They rested on the smooth darkness of empty floor and bare wall.

I stumbled over to the corner, groping with outstretched hands that met only empty space.

Astra's body had gone.

For a moment I had the horrible idea that the old woman had staggered away bent over the knife in her stomach. But that was a crazy idea. Astra had been dead, and dead people couldn't get up and walk away. Obviously Matthew had taken the body elsewhere. But there had been blood on the saddle. My hand was sticky with it.

I crossed the yard again and stood looking up helplessly at the barred and shuttered facade of the house. This had been a proud place once, the grandest house in the village—until my father had denuded it of its valuables and built Moonflete. The shabbiness of Jason Hall was an indictment of my father's ambition. Its locked doors and bolted windows were a sign of—Heather's fear? Fear that the thieves who rode across the moors might break in and steal the motheaten rugs and kitchen cutlery?

Heather was elderly and fretful, but I had not considered her to be a particularly nervous type. Yet Jason Hall was as tightly locked up as if it held a pile of gold. Why? I puzzled, biting my lip, while my common sense urged me to stop bothering about such a minor problem when I was surrounded by so many other greater perils.

Light gleamed from the window of what I assumed was the kitchen. I went across and knocked loudly on the door at the side. It seemed a long time but was in reality only a minute before bolts were drawn back inside and the door opened a cautious inch.

'Who is it? Who's there?' a female voice enquired fearfully.

'Is that Cook or Mary?'

'Who wants to know?' the voice demanded,

'Miss Fletcher—Miss Melody Fletcher.'

'Is that Miss Fletcher from Moonflete?' The door opened wider and a round face appeared in the aperture.

'May I come in?' I asked.

'Oh yes, Miss Fletcher?' She held the door wide enough for me to squeeze through and promptly bolted it behind me.

'Are you Mary?' I enquired.

'Yes, Miss. I'm sorry I was a bit slow coming to the door, but there's only Cook and me here tonight and we get a bit nervous after dark,' she explained, picking a candle from the dresser at the side.

'Has anybody been here tonight?' I asked.

'Why, I couldn't rightly say, Miss. I had my afternoon off today, and I'm afraid I was a bit late getting back. Cook said that Mrs. Broome and Miss Cherry have gone back to Moonflete. Were you wanting something, Miss?'

'I told Mrs. Broome that I would collect some things for her,' I improvised. 'A black fan, some smelling-salts, one or two other things. If you would show me the way to her room I can get them for myself.'

If she thought my request odd, she said nothing but bobbed a curtsey and led me along the passage and up the steps to the main part of the house. The bobbing flame of her candle cast thin shadows on the damp stained walls.

'This is Mrs. Broome's room, Miss,' Mary said, indicating a door close at hand.

'Thank you. I'll need a light.'

'Yes, of course, Miss.' Mary went in and lit some candles, from the flame of her own. 'We were hoping to get oil-lamps but oil's that expensive these days!'

'Thank you, Mary. I won't be very long.'

I closed the door behind her and sat down briefly on the curtained bed. I was like a mouse in a trap, I thought, running round in circles, unable to discover the spring that would open the door. At this moment Uncle Daniel might be approaching Jason Hall, to silence me before Matthew came. And I sat here, like a fool, wondering why Jason Hall was kept so closely locked. I had found the scarf and it had led me to my mother's killer. There was surely nothing here.

I took a fan from the dressing-table and added a small box of notepaper that was near to it. There were no smelling-salts but these would have to suffice, unless there was something in the drawers. But the drawers contained only a few discarded ribbons.

My glance fell on an inner door, half-obscured by a threadbare curtain. The rug near the door had been kicked aside and there were splashes on the floor. I held the candle closer and examined the dark blotches. My own hand was marked with the same stain.

I sat back on my heels and stared down at the floor. Something, somebody had come this way, or had been brought this way. And the saddle of Matthew's horse had been wet with blood.

In a sudden fury, I rose and seized the handle of the door, shaking it violently and then, this proving fruitless, banged upon the wood with my fists.

'Mary! Mary!' I ran out into the passage and called down the echoing well of the stairs.

'Yes, Miss? Were you wanting something?'

Her candle streamed up from below.

'Come up here at once and bring an axe with you!' I ordered.

'A—did you say an *axe*, Miss?'

'Yes, Mary. An axe! There's such a thing in the house, I suppose?'

'There's the one for chopping wood down in the kitchen.'

'Then fetch it up here. Quickly!'

The candle bounced away and I went back into the bedroom, clenching my fists, trying to breathe deeply and evenly to restore my self-control.

Mary panted up the stairs and along the corridor. She was carrying the axe and at any other time the expression on her face would have made me laugh.

'Oh Miss, whatever is it? Whatever do you need an axe for?' she gasped.

'To break down a door,' I said grimly.

'But that door's locked, Miss. Mr. Frank keeps his private papers there,' she argued.

'Does he indeed! Stand back, Mary.'

I took the axe and made a lunge at the door, but the handle weighed down my hand and the blade merely grazed the wood.

'You'll more than likely cut your foot off if you don't mind out,' Mary warned. 'Here, Miss, let me do it!'

She took the axe, flexed her sturdy muscles and sent it with a splintering crash through one of the panels.

'Cook's that deaf she won't hear a blessed thing,' she assured me as I jumped nervously. 'Though what Mr. Frank and Mrs. Broome will say when they see this, I cannot bear to think! But we've never questioned Fletcher doings though I'll never understand—oh, Lord! Oh, Miss! Did you ever see such a thing? Oh, Lord!'

The panel yawned and the shaking candle in my hand illuminated the interior of the small room. Astra's body was huddled in the corner and nearby lay Matthew, eyes closed and face ghastly white.

A voice that didn't sound like my own said calmly, 'Hurry up, Mary! We must get in there at once.'

To her credit she wasted no more time on exclamations but wielded the axe to such good purpose that the door flew inwards and I stepped over to Matthew and knelt, feeling frantically for pulse and heartbeat.

'He's been shot!' Mary said. 'Oh, Miss, whoever could have done it?'

'We have to get a doctor. Can you bring a doctor here, Mary?'

Pulse and heartbeat were still strong but he was bleeding.

'I can run down for Dr. Ferguson,' she said at once.

'Tell him there is an emergency at Jason Hall. Make him hurry.'

I hurried myself to the curtained bed to snatch pillow and blanket. As I lifted Matthew's head, something red as blood but of hard texture gleamed beneath it. It was a ruby earring. The Fleetwood rubies, I thought, and no doubt the Astley silver cups and the Ayres' coins had been kept here too.

'Shall I get Cook, Miss?' Mary was lingering to ask.

'No. Get the doctor. And *hurry!*'

It would take precious minutes to rouse a deaf cook, I thought, and watched anxiously as Mary went without asking any further questions though I was certain her head was buzzing with them.

The bleeding now was no more than a trickle and I could only pray that the bullet had missed any vital part. I fixed my eyes on his unconscious face, averting them from the huddled, shrivelled thing in the corner, and settled myself to wait. In my anxiety I had pushed out of my conscious mind the terror of Uncle Daniel's admission of guilt and his voice shouting after me from the threshold of Moonflete.

Mary must have run at top speed down the drive and through the unlit street, for I heard her voice below and heavier footsteps ascending the stairs before I had begun to worry about the passage of time.

The doctor was a short, spare man, one of those who had stared at me in church the previous Sunday. He carried his bag and favoured me with a brisk, unsmiling nod before he knelt down by Matthew.

After a few minutes, he spoke as if he were

quite accustomed to being called out to tend gunshot wounds and view corpses in the middle of the night.

'The bullet will need to be extracted. I'll require clean towels and hot water. Get them for me, there's a good girl, Mary. And I'll need your help to move him to the bed afterwards.'

'Is he going to die?' I whispered.

'Not for another thirty or forty years,' said Dr. Ferguson. 'Matthew Fletcher is as strong as a bull. Whoever fired aimed too high for the heart.'

He rose, dusting his hands and went over to the body in the corner. Mary had gone out again, her face a study in excitement. I guessed that nothing so thrilling as the events of this night had ever happened in her life before.

'There's nothing to be done for the old lady,' the doctor informed me. 'What in the world possessed her to take her own life?'

'Take her own—wasn't she murdered?'

'Not very likely, judging from the angle of the knife. Of course, I'd need to make a detailed examination, but I'd reckon on suicide. Are there any more patients lying around?' he enquired wryly.

'I'm sorry. You must need some explanation.'

'The local magistrate and the Coroner will,' he returned. 'My business is with undoing other folks' mischief. I can tell you I'm not a whit surprised. Ever since Eben Fletcher brought that slant-eyed yellow girl and set the neighbourhood buzzing I've been expecting trouble of one kind or another. But Matthew is a good lad for all he's a Fletcher.'

Mary had come back with towels over her arm and the doctor turned back to his patient. I stood uncertainly in the background.

'There's nothing for you to do here, young lady. Mary will be of more help to me,' he said to me, somewhat brusquely.

'I'll come back as soon as I can.'

I cast one swift glance at the greenish-white face and still form and went out again through the shabby bedroom and into the dark corridor. I was upheld by a mixture of anger and determination. I was past fear, past caring whether Uncle Daniel was still waiting for me or had followed me. I had sent Matthew to find Astra's body and he had been shot. My anger was directed partly against myself, for I had shown my trust by sending him, however inadvertently, into danger.

I let myself out through the kitchen door and came round to the front of the house again. Dark as it was, enough light was shed from the scudding clouds and pale moon to illuminate the steep moorland road.

It was colder; the wind bruised my cheek and the silk trousers and tunic were no protection. I folded my arms and bent my head into the wind, feeling it tangle my loosened hair.

141

Somewhere beyond the rise thunder growled and Moonflete was streaked momentarily with the blue-white of a lightning flash.

The front door was ajar. Yang was evidently too worried about Astra to attend conscientiously to his duties. I slipped within the great hall and stood for a moment, listening, but though the rooms were bright with lamps and candles I could hear nothing. Why should the house be so brilliantly lit?

A murmur of voices from along the corridor broke into my train of thought. The others were still in the flower-filled garden room, talking, apparently oblivious of my own comings and goings.

There were two silver mounted pistols on the wall below the stained glass of the upper window. I took one down cautiously and held it in my hand. I had no idea whether it was loaded or not, and I was quite certain that I could never bring myself to fire the weapon, but it gave me a sense of security just to possess it.

Then I went softly down the corridor and pushed wide the door. Stephen looked up casually from his newspaper, then lowered it and stared at me agape. Frank who was seated on the arm of his mother's chair broke off his whispering to stare at me too. I suppose I must have presented an alarming sight with my hair straggling over my shoulders, the tunic and trousers grimed and streaked with blood, and the big pistol clutched awkwardly in my hand.

'Melody? What the devil has been happening?'

It was Stephen who spoke, pushing aside his newspaper.

'A great deal,' I said shakily. 'Where's Cherry?'

'In her room, I suppose. She said something about an early night.'

'Where's Uncle Daniel?'

'He followed you out. We heard him calling after you,' Stephen said. 'Melody, where have you been?'

'Uncle Daniel killed my mother. By now he'll be trying to escape,' I said.

'*Daniel*? Oh, but surely—' Heather fell silent biting her lip.

'I'd better go to the nearest magistrate and get a warrant sworn. Melody, are you sure it was Uncle Daniel?' Stephen asked.

'He told me so,' I said flatly.

'Fleetwood is the nearest,' Frank said.

'Then I'll go there. Frank, stay with the ladies.'

In his haste he had forgotten to enquire Matthew's whereabouts, but I held out my hand as he brushed past me.

'Take this to him. It belongs to his wife.'

Stephen gave the stone a surprised and puzzled look.

Frank, seeing the gleam of ruby, spoke

143

sharply.

'Where did you find that?'

'At Jason Hall,' I said, and there was a crack as one of Heather's knitting needles snapped in half.

CHAPTER TWELVE

'At Jason Hall!' Stephen exclaimed. 'Why did you go down there? Melody, what the devil is going on? Where's Matthew all this time?'

I opened my mouth to reply and felt, rather than saw, the anguished pleading of Heather's glance.

'Matthew is—busy,' I said at last. 'It's best for you to ride over to the Fleetwood house.'

'It's the best part of a two hour ride,' Stephen said, still looking at the ruby in his palm. 'And by the time Mrs. Fleetwood has recovered from her transports of joy another hour will have passed. It'll be the early hours of the morning before I get back.'

'Frank will look after us. Uncle Daniel won't return now that I know about him,' I said quickly. 'And the Fleetwoods will be pleased to get back one of the rubies.'

'There's a reward out,' Stephen reflected and his shallow, handsome face brightened with interest. The prospect of gaining a little profit was of more importance to him than the revelation of his uncle's guilt. I had been right to compare Stephen to the surface of the sea for his nature was a blank as water.

'You'd better hurry,' I said again, and he nodded and went out, still clutching the ruby.

'Do you have to wave that gun about?' Heather asked querulously. She had recovered herself a little and was taking refuge in attack.

'I feel safer with it,' I said coldly.

'You went to Jason Hall and found—the ruby?' Frank asked.

His handsome young face had paled, and his eyes darted about the room.

'It was under Matthew's head,' I said, and Heather half-rose in her chair and cried out in a trembling voice.

'Matthew's head? Oh, my God! Frank, you haven't—you didn't?'

'It was an accident,' Frank said sulkily. 'I heard someone in the shed when I got back to Jason Hall. I thought it was—well, never mind who I thought it was—and I fired. Then I discovered it was Matthew, and Astra's body was there too.'

'Astra is dead!' Heather's voice was a terrified whisper.

'I found her body earlier this afternoon and told Matthew about it,' I said shortly.

'I didn't know what to do,' Frank said. 'Matthew wasn't dead but he was bleeding badly and he hadn't seen who'd shot him. I found his horse tethered outside the back wall and I managed to get him into the saddle but he keeled over and the horse galloped off.'

'So you let yourself into Jason Hall and dragged him up to that little room next to your mother's bedroom,' I said bitterly.

'It was hard work, getting him up the stairs,' Frank said as if he expected me to sympathise. 'Cook's deaf as a post, but she might have come walking in from the kitchen at any moment and Mary was due back from her afternoon out. But I managed it, and then I thought I'd better put Astra's body there too. She was small and light but it was no pleasant task.'

'You should have called a doctor,' Heather scolded. 'You should have gone for help.'

'And have the authorities poking about Jason Hall? No, mother, I couldn't.'

'You couldn't risk it, could you?' I said, and the pistol was power in my hands. 'You couldn't risk anyone's attention being focused on Jason Hall, in case they discovered the stolen property! And you, Heather, you knew about it.'

'I never knew for certain,' she said miserably. 'I suspected, but I wasn't sure. Frank kept the key of the little room, but I never asked questions. I let him be.'

'To rob all the neighbours? How convenient for you!' I began, but she overrode me, her voice strident.

'Neighbours? *Neighbours*! Fine neighbours

to sit tamely by while my own father gambled and drank away our property so that when he died Eben Fletcher could step in and buy up everything. The Fletchers always envied the Jasons.'

'My father let you stay on at Jason Hall,' I reminded her.

'So kind of him!' Heather mocked and her sallow face twisted with rage. 'So kind of the great Eben Fletcher to let me stay on as unpaid housekeeper for his own jumped-up family.'

'Then why did you stay if you were so proud?' I demanded.

'Because I hoped that one day Eben might—marry me!' she said, and gave a convulsive movement of her hands that sent the tattered remnants of her knitting flying to the ground.

'Mother?' Frank looked at her in consternation.

'He was older than I was, but I thought if he married me I could be mistress of Jason Hall again,' she said, twisting her swollen hands together. 'It wasn't such a far-fetched notion. I was quite a pretty girl in those days. There were several gentlemen, but there! I had no dowry after my father's death. And I hoped, I so hoped, that Eben might decide to—but he didn't. *He didn't*! He went away on one of his trading voyages and came back with a Chinese wife. *Chinese*!'

Her eyes were venomous.

'You loved my father?' I stared at her, trying to imagine Heather Broome as a younger woman eager for love.

'I wanted to be mistress of Jason Hall again,' she said sullenly. 'I wanted to be Mrs. Fletcher of Jason Hall, but Eben brought home another wife. A girl of eighteen! And he was already past fifty! Nobody ever dreamed that he would marry. It was indecent; indecent!'

'But you married,' I pointed out.

'One of my old suitors,' she nodded, 'who didn't care that I had no dowry. I married him and he was very kind to me, but I was cheated even there. He died of the typhus six months before his son was born. I wish you had known your father, Frank. He was very good to me.'

'My father was good to you, too,' I reminded her stonily. 'He gave Jason Hall back to you upon your marriage.'

'Because he no longer had any use for it himself,' said Heather. 'Jason Hall wasn't good enough for his beautiful Chinese bride. So he built another house at the very top of the hill. A house that could be seen from the moors around, from the valley and the village. Moonflete, symbol of Eben Fletcher's rise to power and success!'

'My mother's right,' said Frank. 'I was reared on Fletcher charity. Do you think that's pleasant? Do you think I enjoyed seeing my mother patronised, being allowed to share a tutor with that spoilt nit-wit Cherry, being invited up to the "big house" as a privilege? I loathed it for myself and for my mother, and there was nothing to be done.'

'You could have tried work!' I snapped.

'At what? I was brought up to be a gentleman,' he said. 'Oh, I might have made my way in the mill, but that was closed down when I was still a child. There was nothing for me to do in this place, and I couldn't leave my mother to face the Fletchers alone.'

'So you started to rob the houses around?'

'About a year ago, for a wager, some friends dared me to take some coins that old Colonel Ayres was forever boasting about. They agreed to create a diversion by riding their horses and flashing lights up and down one part of the valley while I slipped over to the Colonel's house and calmly filched the coins!'

'But if it was a wager, dear, you could have given them back and explained that it was a joke,' Heather said feebly.

'Why should I give them back after the trouble I'd taken?' her son demanded. 'The fellows who helped me agreed to help me again and to keep quiet—for a consideration. It was so easy, Melody. People always forget to bolt one little door even when they think they're most prepared against thieves, and as a young gentleman I was welcome in every house.'

'And could return the hospitality you were shown by noting the position of the locks and the location of the valuables? How clever of you! But why not Moonflete?' I asked him. 'There are beautiful things at Moonflete. Why didn't you help yourself to a few things here?'

'I—couldn't,' Frank said uneasily.

'Because of Eben Fletcher? That was it, wasn't it?' I said. 'You were afraid of my father, afraid of what he might do if he ever discovered that you had stolen anything from him. So you kept your hands off Moonflete.'

'I always hoped that Frank and Cherry would marry one day,' Heather said with a touch of wistfulness.

'Marry that simpering goldilocks who has no thought in her head beyond what to wear to church that will make people look at her! I've told you before that I'll not consider it, Mother,' Frank said violently. 'And there's no sense in pressing it, now that Cherry will never inherit Moonflete anyway.'

Moonflete, I thought. Always Moonflete! The great house at the top of the hill had been cause and symbol of so much pride, so much greed and so much hatred. And the house had awakened the same qualities in myself. I had been pleased to discover that my childhood home was a beautiful and wealthy one. I had coveted the lovely clothes that had belonged to my mother, and I had hated the thought of anyone trying to get them away from me. In

150

the descriptions of Eben Fletcher with his vaunting ambition and his possessiveness I recognised something of myself, and the recognition frightened me.

Heather said with desperate and ugly pleading, 'Let Frank go free. Let him leave here, now tonight! Please, Melody, don't force him to wait here until Stephen gets back with the magistrate.'

'He's a thief,' I said hotly, 'and a murderer in intention if nothing else. Matthew could have bled to death while you sat here.'

'I meant to ride off as soon as Stephen was out of the way,' Frank said. 'I would have told my mother about Matthew. I swear it, Melody. I never killed anyone.'

'Let him go free,' Heather said again and her swollen hand clutched the edge of my crumpled tunic twisting the soft silk while she stared up at me in anguish.

The pistol in my hand was heavy. My wrist was beginning to ache.

'You can keep all the things,' Frank said, his face twitching nervously. 'I brought them up from Jason Hall and I put them in a chest in the library. I was going to say good-bye to my mother and tell her about Matthew, and then I was going to sell them in Manchester—and disappear.'

Suddenly I was tired to death of both of them. Heather's fretful pleading, her son's weakness and feeble excuses grated on me.

Matthew whom I loved had been shot and might be even more badly hurt than I knew. Astra who had loved me for my mother's sake was dead. Suicide, the doctor had said. *Suicide*? But Uncle Daniel had had to kill her surely, because she knew of his connection with Silver Moon's death?

'I have a little money of my own,' Heather was saying. 'It would buy Frank a passage on a ship. If he could get to Liverpool ahead of the magistrate, he'd stand some sort of chance.'

'You'd better bring me the things that you stole. I'll see that they're returned to their rightful owners with some kind of explanation,' I said wearily.

Frank darted out of the room and Heather looked at me dully.

'You're very kind,' she said. 'That's what makes the Fletchers so damnable! There's a streak of genuine kindness in them all.'

'Not in me,' I said harshly. 'There's no kindness in me towards you or your son. I despise you both for staying on here, for letting my father use you both as if he owned you. At least he gave Frank an education. If he had had an ounce of character Frank would have used his education to make something of himself, instead of robbing his neighbours. And if you cared so much for your son you should have made him leave you instead of keeping him here and dangling Cherry in front of him as a possible wife!'

I sat down abruptly, my anger dried up for Heather was weeping noisily.

'It wasn't only the house,' she gulped. 'I hoped for so long that Eben would marry me. He was a handsome man, older than I was, I know, but with such presence! Such a commanding manner! But nobody believed that he ever would marry. He was past fifty when he went on his last trading voyage and I hoped that he would settle down and make me his wife when he returned.'

'And instead he brought back Silver Moon.'

'Young enough to be his daughter,' she muttered, and her mouth trembled.

'The things are all here,' Frank said, coming back into the room with a leather bag in his hand and a sulky expression on his face. 'The rubies and the coins and some rather nice silver from the Mortons.'

His fingers clung reluctantly to the leather bag, as if he regretted having to give up the proceeds of the only independent actions of his life.

'Take your mother back to Jason Hall,' I ordered. 'She can finance your journey to Liverpool, for I'll not burden you with any more Fletcher charity. Your own horse must be in the stables. Mount your mother on one of the others. And don't,' I added, 'tell me that you're grateful. Don't ever insult me with that word. I'm doing this merely to get rid of you both.'

153

Heather reached for her stick and leaned on it more heavily than I had seen her do before. She had aged since learning of the thefts of her son and I felt a treacherous pity mingle with my dislike.

Frank dropped the bag into an armchair and let his eyes linger on it wistfully for a moment or two.

'Tell the doctor at Jason Hall that Frank found the stolen property and is off to the magistrates,' I began.

'A doctor? You sent for a doctor for Matthew?' Heather faltered.

'I didn't leave him to bleed to death!' I snapped.

Their continued presence was an intolerable burden. Weak and useless, both of them, I thought viciously. I wanted to be rid of them so that I could find more evidence against Uncle Daniel—evidence I could present to the magistrate when Stephen came back with him.

The possibility that Uncle Daniel might return before anybody else and silence me, was a nagging fear in my mind. But even with Frank and Heather gone I wouldn't be alone in the house, and I had the pistol and enough wit, I trusted, to talk my way out of a dangerous situation. There was, I reflected, a great deal of my father's determination in me even if I resembled in looks the frail Silver Moon.

'I'll do everything I can for Matthew, as soon as I've got Frank safely away,' Heather said. 'Your associates won't talk about anything that has occurred, will they, Frank?'

'They're riff-raff, drinking companions,' he said, carelessly. 'They know better than to run their own necks into a noose.'

I let them go without farewell. Of course I would have to see Heather again and try to make unobtrusive reparation for the way in which my father had treated her, but now they were out of Moonflete and I was glad of it.

I took a firmer hold of the pistol and stepped out into the brilliantly lit corridor.

CHAPTER THIRTEEN

There was comparative security within doors, for somewhere beyond the walls Uncle Daniel still loomed like a figure from a half-remembered nightmare of my childhood. I hoped that he was, at this moment, making his escape across the moors and that he had not waited, hiding somewhere, for my return to the house.

As I began to mount the stairs Yang came forward from the direction of the kitchens and bowed, his face screwed up with anxiety.

'Please, Missy,' he asked, 'is it true that Astra is dead? Mr. Stephen said it was so, as he rode away.'

'I'm afraid it is, Yang,' I said regretfully.

'But how, Missy? Astra was old but she was strong. How did she die?' he asked.

'The doctor said that Astra killed herself,' I told him.

'So!' His voice was a long drawn breath.

'Do you know why Astra should do such a thing?' I enquired. 'Why should she?'

'Because she wished to die,' Yang said with gentle and unanswerable logic.

'I'm going upstairs for a while. Will you tell me at once if Mr. Daniel comes in?' I asked.

'Are you going to bed, Missy?'

I shook my head. There would be no sleep for me until I had found proof positive of Uncle Daniel's guilt—proof that I could lay before a magistrate. So far I had only his unsupported word, given to me when no witnesses were present. Astra had killed herself after she learned of it. Some thought, vague, unexpressed, floated at this point almost to the surface of my brain but had evaporated before I could grasp it.

I hesitated outside Uncle Daniel's door, filled with a sudden, absurd nervousness as if I expected him to be lying in wait for me behind the door.

I summoned up my resolution and carefully opened the door wide, resisting the impulse to look apprehensively round the corner of it.

The bedroom, its original decor spoiled by

Uncle Daniel's hearty sporting trophies, was quite empty though the lamps were lit and a fire already laid in the hearth. The room was neat with no signs of any hasty packing. I hoped that signified that Uncle Daniel had rushed away without returning to destroy anything that might point to his guilt.

To deliberately search through another's personal possessions was not one of the habits ingrained in me by Miss Trimlett's upbringing, but I must forget my governess and my former ladylike existence until my own position was secure. So I began, with slow thoroughness to look through every drawer, cupboard and pocket. It was useless!

After half an hour I sat back on my heels, discouraged, and felt a prickling along my spine as a board behind me creaked.

'What in the world are you doing in my father's room?' Cherry demanded.

I felt so stupidly guilty that I could only stammer a reply.

'Why are you dressed? I thought you were in bed.'

'I went up early, with a headache, but it's impossible to sleep properly with folk rushing up and down stairs,' she returned sulkily. 'I got up again a few minutes ago. Where is my father? He vanished directly supper was over and ran out calling for you. Where is he and why are you prying into his belongings?'

'Your father's gone,' I said, rising to my feet.

'Gone where? What are you talking about?' she demanded, fretfully.

'Cherry, it was Uncle Daniel—your father—who killed my mother. He told me so,' I began.

'My father killed your—it's not true,' she broke in angrily. ' I simply don't believe it! It's the most complete nonsense I ever heard in my life. My father doesn't kill people.'

'He admitted it to me. He admitted it to Astra, too. That's why she—'

I stopped, remembering that Cherry didn't know about Astra.

'That's why she what? Where does Astra fit into this rigmarole?'

'She found out that your father had killed my mother and she went to the shed at the back of Jason Hall and killed herself,' I said, too unhappy and impatient to be bothered to break the news gently.

'Astra is dead?'

Cherry sat down abruptly on a stool and looked up at me with tears welling in her blue eyes.

I remembered with compunction that Astra had sometimes taken care of Cherry when she was smaller and that she was in the habit of meeting her once a week.

I put out my hand towards my cousin but she shook it off and jumped up again, scrubbing at her eyes with a scrap of handkerchief and sobbing indignantly.

'Astra wouldn't kill herself because my

father had done anything! Why do you keep saying these terrible things? My father never killed anybody—not your mother, not anybody! I won't believe it! And I won't stay here while you say these things. You haven't given me any proof at all!'

'I'm looking for it now. That's why I'm here.'

My sympathy hardened into rage at her stupidity.

'Proof that Father murdered Silver Moon? Then you *are* crazy,' she cried scornfully. 'I'll tell Matthew what you said. He may not have much in common with my father but he'll not stand by and watch you slander him, accuse him of ridiculous crimes for which there's no proof!'

'I'm looking for it,' I gritted.

'But you haven't found any, have you?' she gibed. 'Well, take your time. Look *at* everything, *into* everything, *behind* everything! You have my permission, cousin Melody. Search! Here, take this box. My father keeps cravats in it, I think.'

She flung a casket at me but it fell short of its target and spilled out in a waterfall of bright and rippling silks.

'Tear the room apart,' she invited sarcastically. 'You'll find no proof that my father ever did anything wrong. I'm going to find Matthew and tell him all the horrible things you've said. We'll see if he likes you quite so much after that.'

'Likes me? Matthew likes me?'

How foolish to let my heart leap with pleasure in the midst of such a chaos of feeling!

'Likes you? He's never taken his eyes off you since you arrived,' Cherry retorted. 'But he'll never let you know it for fear you imagine he wants your inheritance.'

'He's at Jason Hall,' I said, tired of her spitefulness. 'Go and tell him all about me if you choose, and if you meet Uncle Daniel on the way there tell him that he'd better run as far and as fast as possible because I'll find the proof I need.'

Cherry gave a furious, incoherent exclamation and whirled out of the room. My legs suddenly shook beneath me with weariness and tension. I had been talking nonsense and I knew it, for there was no further proof. Only the blue scarf, only the fear in Uncle Daniel's eyes when they rested on my moonstone necklace, linked him with the death of Silver Moon. There was no evidence at all that I could present to a magistrate. Astra had known, but Astra was dead.

I went out of the room unsteadily, leaning momentarily against the wall as I made my way along the corridor. I had lived through too much in too short a time. The events of the past days were beginning to overwhelm me at the very moment when I needed to be completely clearheaded, to protect myself.

The house was so quiet that I could hear my own breathing below the occasional gusts of wind that shook the windows. Cherry would be running wildly down the steep path, bent on telling Matthew what a despicable creature I was.

Heather would be at Jason Hall and Frank would have ridden away to evade the magistrate Stephen was bringing with him, and Uncle Daniel was—on his way to escape as well? Or in the house, waiting until I was alone? Moonflete was locked securely at night, but the front door had still been ajar when I came back from Jason Hall. Uncle Daniel could have returned earlier by the same route.

And I was alone.

In panic I hurried to the top of the stairs and called down.

'Yang! Yang!'

'You wished for something, Missy?' His voice came from the end of the upper corridor as he emerged from my own bedroom.

'I have lit the fire for Missy. It was Astra's task,' he informed me gravely. 'If you will be needing anything more, please to tell me.'

'I need a bath,' I said ruefully, 'but it will take time to heat the water, I suppose.'

'The kitchen fire is low, but in an hour, two hours—'

'Never mind! I'll stay dirty,' I said flippantly,

but my humour was evidently not appreciated.

'Missy is always most pure, most clean,' Yang said at once.

'Where are the other servants?' I asked.

'The coachman went with Mr. Stephen, and the grooms are in their quarters over the stables. I cannot be certain where the others are. Astra and I never mingle with English domestics,' he said haughtily.

'Will you make quite certain that the doors are locked?' I enquired nervously.

'Yes, Missy.'

'And leave all the lamps burning, I'm expecting Mr. Stephen.'

'The lights will burn all night as custom decrees,' he bowed. 'Will Missy come down to wait in the garden room? I will be most pleased to make tea.'

'I'll follow you down,' I said absently and the thought that had eluded me before nibbled again at the edges of my mind. It continued to nag at me as I went into my room with some idea of changing my clothes in readiness for the magistrate's arrival.

Lights burning as custom decreed? But what custom? And so many lights? When I had returned earlier, Moonflete had been ablaze with lamps. Even Uncle Daniel's room had glared, shadowless. And on my first evening too there had been lamps everywhere; on tables, windowsills, even in the hearth of the library where my father's body had lain.

Lights lit according to custom? According to *funeral* custom? Lights for my father, lights for Astra? But the lamps had been kindled this evening before anyone at Moonflete knew about Astra's death. Someone had known before I gave the news. It must have been Uncle Daniel but the doctor said Astra had killed herself. What was it that Cherry had said? 'Astra would never kill herself because my father had murdered Silver Moon.' No, I thought, if Astra had discovered Uncle Daniel to be the killer of her beloved Silver Moon she would have laid information against him. She would never have killed herself.

But Uncle Daniel had admitted his own guilt to me. *Hadn't he*?

I heard the echo of that brief conversation in the dining room.

'You were the one. It was you.'

'It was. Eben suspected it but never could be certain. I was a fool to keep the scarf. It was at the back of the drawer and I thought it was safe enough, but I should have destroyed it long ago. Long ago.'

'Astra knew. Astra guessed.'

'She told me so, on the way to Jason Hall.'

A blue scarf, delicate and feminine, kept for years as a souvenir. A moonstone necklace that had appeared mysteriously in the garden of my London home. My father had died, gasping out moonstones. Astra and Uncle Daniel had both been terrified by their

163

appearance. Lights burning according to custom for a dead man.

Silver Moon with her yellow skin and tiny, useless feet. Bonfires lit to burn the rotted trees in the copse. Silver Moon, wed to an elderly man, amusing herself in her loneliness by teasing a boy into desire. Uncle Daniel keeping a blue scarf for nearly twenty years.

Eben suspected it but never could be certain.

Uncle Daniel must have been a fine figure of a man until he began to drink. 'She laughed and told me how silly I was to think she could feel anything for a young barbarian.' Matthew had said that. Silver Moon had no use for young men of her own generation. She had been bored by a man past fifty. Eighteen years before Uncle Daniel had been in his thirties, neither an old man nor a callow boy.

I could no longer bear to stay in that beautiful white room. It was becoming a prison as it had been a prison for my mother. The moonstone collar was tight, chokingly tight.

I wrenched at the clasp and the lovely silver chain with its attendant stones coiled over my hand. Given to me by unknown hands on my eighteenth birthday.

I opened the drawer of the dragon-carved cabinet and dropped the jewels within, slamming the drawer shut as if I wanted to shut my mother's memory away with it. But that was impossible. Silver Moon's blood ran in my veins, when I looked in the mirror I saw her face, and something of her subtlety had descended to me.

I would wash my face and go downstairs. The magistrate would be here at any moment. He must come soon, very soon, for I was no longer certain who or where my enemies could be.

The door leading to the bathroom was locked. Frowning, I opened the little cupboard in the wall where my own set of keys was kept. Emptiness gazed at me as I looked down. Yang had told me that a bath could be made ready in one or two hours. Why then did light stream from beneath the door? And why, as I stood there, did my ears catch faint footsteps within?

I was truly frightened now, so frightened that my mouth was dry and the heavy pistol in my clenched hand shook as if it were a branch of aspen.

I must find Yang and get him to open the door. But Yang had gone downstairs to make tea, and Yang was an old man. It would be better for me to creep out of the house now and hide somewhere until Stephen came. Or I could rouse the other servants, though I was not sure where they slept, or even how many of them were in residence.

I backed away from the door, my ears strained to catch the shuffling from within, but the noise had ceased. I sensed that like me, my unseen adversary was holding his breath.

I edged to the outer door, to the door

165

leading to the corridor, and heard my own voice whispering, 'Yang, Yang?' then swelling into a scream of terror. '*Yang*! Yang, come here! I order you to come here!'

A key turned softly in the bathroom door and Yang came out, pulling the door close beside him.

'What are you doing in there?' I quavered. 'Why was the door locked? Where are the keys?'

'I am beginning to prepare Missy's bath as you requested,' he said.

'I told you that I'd changed my mind,' I said angrily. 'But I do need to wash my face.'

'Better for Missy to wait for hot water,' he returned.

'I'll manage with cold water,' I said, but the old servant had put his arm across the space.

'Better to wait for hot water,' he repeated. 'One hour, two hours.'

I lifted the pistol and pointed it towards him, as my voice came, calm and authoritative.

'Stand aside. I order you to stand aside.'

'Missy will not understand,' he began, but the habit of obedience was too deeply ingrained in him for he stood aside with bowed head, folding his arms within the wide sleeves of his tunic. And I marched into the lovely mirror-lined room, where every surface of shining glass reflected the heavily built, middle-aged man who lay in Silver Moon's sunken bath.

166

'Mr. Daniel was a bad man,' said Yang sadly. 'He dishonoured Madam Silver Moon.'

'Dishonoured? Not murdered?'

'He brought shame upon her as she brought shame upon the master's house,' said Yang. 'As an honourable man it was my duty to punish.'

'To—punish!'

'To execute,' said Yang. 'Such is the custom of the house.'

'*You* killed Silver Moon?'

'Executed her, Missy, as I promised her father I would do if she proved false to the rich merchant who made her his bride,' Yang returned calmly, and gave me a little bow as if he had enquired if I needed a cup of tea.

CHAPTER FOURTEEN

For a full minute, I believe, I stood staring at the old man while words and actions settled into a pattern in my mind.

'Tell it to me from the beginning. Mr. Daniel was Silver Moon's lover? Is that what you're saying?'

'The master was very good,' said Yang. 'He brought Astra and me with him out of China when he wed Silver Moon. But the Madam was young and foolish and would not submit to her husband. She paid him no respect but treated him with great discourtesy. Her father charged me, before she wed, to guard the honour of his house for he feared lest his daughter stain it.'

'And she took a lover?'

'Madam Silver Moon was very young,' he said sadly. 'She was happy here at first, happy until after her child was born. But Astra took good care of you, Missy, and there was little for the Madam to do. She stayed long hours in her room and would call in those whom she wished to bear her company. But she was not happy and when people are not happy they grow cruel and hard.'

'When did you find out that she had a lover?' I asked.

'On the night of the big bonfires, when the trees were cut down. Late that night I was called to her room. She told me that I must saddle a horse for her use. I told her, Missy, that I must first ask the master for leave to do such a thing. But she laughed, Missy. She told me that if I asked the master she would deny it all and swear that I lied to cause trouble between them.'

'Did you saddle the horse?'

'I said I would obey if she would tell me why she needed to ride so late at night. But she laughed at me again, Missy. She said I was a fool to ask her such a thing when with my own eyes I could see that she was young and her husband was old. She told me that she had a man who would make her happy. She called him the best of the Fletchers and said she would go away with him that night. I begged her, Missy. I begged her not to stain the honour of her father or the honour of her husband but she mocked at honour. She mocked at the old ways.'

'So you killed her?'

'It was necessary, Missy, for I must do as my old master had ordered. He knew of the weakness in his daughter and feared for her. But she died swiftly. She died very swiftly, Missy, with the thrust of a knife, in the old way, according to custom.'

'And you put her on the bonfire?' I realised.

'I carried her down the outer stairs and through the yard to the burning trees, Missy. And I took the moonstones from her neck so they must come to you when you were eighteen.'

'Tell me about the moonstones,' I invited.

If I could keep him here talking for long enough, somebody would come. I could only assume they had stopped off at Jason Hall, and I prayed silently that they would come soon.

'The necklace is ancient, Missy. For many generations it is passed down from mother to eldest daughter on the eighteenth year of her birth. The custom is an old one; the moonstones bring good fortune. Madam Silver Moon was given them by her father when she wed the master.'

'And you took them from her neck and kept them to give to me? It was you who put them in the bird tray in the garden?'

'I knew where you lived, Missy. When I returned to the house that night the master came to me very late to tell me Madam Silver Moon had gone. He feared for your own safety, Missy, and bade me take you to the widow woman and then far away to London.'

'My father hated me,' I said bleakly.

'I fear so, Missy, for he knew the nature of Madam Silver Moon, and suspected that she loved another man. But he could not be certain of the lover's name. He could not even be certain that she was dead.'

'So he reared me as bait for the day when he could bring me here, and trap my mother's lover and possible killer.'

'We all went down to London in the month of January which proved most fortunate, for I was able to slip away and give your gift in a most secret manner, according to custom.'

'My father cried out the words "moonstones" during his last heart attack,' I remembered.

'He sent for me, Missy, to tell me that you were coming here, to tell me what to do in presenting you to the family. It was then that I made a most foolish mistake, most foolish, but I am older now and my mind is not as bright as it used to be.'

'You told him that you had given me the

necklace?' I prompted.

'Yes, Missy. Madam Silver Moon did not wear jewels, but this necklace lay always beneath the collar of her tunic. The master knew of it for she believed that it would bring her good fortune. The man who was her lover would know of it too. Mr. Daniel recognised it when you wore it at supper. I saw the knowledge in his eyes as I served the meal. To the others it meant nothing.'

'Astra recognised it too. She guessed then that you had given it to me, for my eighteenth birthday.'

'Astra was greatly troubled in her mind. She was foolish, not understanding that I had to follow the old master's orders. That is why she killed herself, Missy. To take the sin of her brother upon her own soul.'

'Brother?'

'Astra was born my sister, Missy. We both grew up in the household of the old master. Its customs were our customs and its honour was our honour.'

'You followed Uncle Daniel,' I said slowly, 'and struck him down on the path after he ran calling after me.'

'I took upon myself the vengeance that would have been the master's if he had lived,' Yang said.

'And dragged him up here through the yard to hide him until you could remove the body.'

'It is the room where only you might go. I

meant to hide him away, Missy, so deep and safe that he would never be found. But I am older than I was before and Mr. Daniel is a heavy man, very difficult to drag away.'

He looked at his gnarled hands and sighed, as if he regretted the swift passage of time more than anything else.

'And now you will have to kill me too,' I said slowly.

'But why should I do that?' the old man asked. 'Your honour is unstained, Missy. Why should I do something so wicked to one who is a true daughter of her father's house?'

'But I will inform on you to the magistrates. In this country the laws and customs are different,' I said. 'It is forbidden to kill a dishonourable wife or her lover. You knew that very well else you wouldn't have tried to hide your part in the deed.'

'I have done nothing against honour,' Yang said, and there was a ragged dignity in his bearing. 'I have kept the ancient laws of my master's house, paid respects to the dead with the lighting of many lamps, even for Mr. Daniel. I know these matters are not understood in this cold country, but you are the daughter of Silver Moon, of her blood.'

'And being of her blood must avenge her murder for whatever reason she was killed,' I said steadily. 'They will hang you for murder, Yang. That is the custom in this land, and we must follow the customs.'

172

I had reached the outer door and my hand scrabbled for the knob. But Yang was coming slowly towards me and on his face was an expression of deep regret. Had he, I wondered, looked like that just before he killed Silver Moon?

'If you kill me, Yang, you will bring dishonour upon this house,' I said.

'They take no heed of customs here,' said Yang. 'And you have not understood, Missy, for you are half-Fletcher and not bred in the ancient ways.'

I raised the pistol but he kept advancing towards me and his many reflections kept pace with him. I closed my eyes and tugged frantically at the trigger but the expected flash never came. The weapon was quite obviously useless. And Yang was almost upon me, yellowed hands outstretched.

I threw the pistol wildly in his face and fled down the narrow stone steps into the yard. The kitchen door was open and I ran through the long room with its glowing range, past the sculleries into the main hall where I wrestled furiously with the bolts.

I could hear footsteps on the upper landing now, but the last bolt was almost drawn. It slid back with a little click and I stooped to lift the latch as a rush of air fanned my cheek and a knife quivered in the wooden panel where my head had been a split second before.

Yang stood on the stairs and in his face now

was only the look of a man determined on self-preservation, with all thoughts of custom and honour gone.

I swung back the door and ran down the wide steps to the gravel path. My mother had not been able to run on her bound feet but had been killed, not for property, not even out of hatred, but for the sake of a barbaric tradition.

But I could run, hearing the footsteps gaining on me. I could run through the driving wind that swept across the high grass above the deep valley.

And then arms enfolded me, and riders surrounded me, and through a grey mist I heard Matthew's voice.

'Are you hurt, Melody? Darling, are you hurt?'

That was long ago and he has spoken many words of love to me since, but none have rung so sweetly in my ears as that softly urgent query.

There was confusion then and a bustle of people and a series of horrified exclamations as Yang, pausing on the steps with the knife wrenched from the door in his hand, made a gesture almost of resignation and turned the weapon upon himself.

It happened a long time ago but it was many months before I could stand without fear on the gravel path that led up to the main door. The thin dark silhouette of the old man still, in my imagination, crumpled slowly over the threshold against the background of the brightly lighted hall.

For a long time afterwards the echoes of hatred rumbled about the high white walls. But those fancies came when I was alone.

For the next few days I seemed never to have one minute to myself. Moonflete was filled with the living and the dead. Matthew, whose insistence upon returning despite his wound made my heart glow, had been ordered to bed, and Heather came to act as nurse, for Cherry was too scatterbrained, and I was too shy to be of any use.

I had never felt shyness on Matthew's account before, but now I hesitated before his room and then went past without knocking.

I was needed in half a dozen places at once. I had never realised that death could bring so many arrangements to be made, so many people to see, so many papers to sign.

My most difficult interview was with Mr. Fleetwood. On the morning of Uncle Daniel's funeral, the shrewd-faced magistrate drove up to the house in his carriage, with Mr. Briggs sitting nervously at his side. Cherry was in her room, weeping dutifully as she tried to make up her mind which of two black bonnets was the most attractive. Stephen had gone down to the church to make the final arrangements with the Vicar and Heather, whom I had glimpsed briefly on the stairs, had vanished in the direction of Matthew's room.

I received my visitors alone in the garden room, enduring the lawyer's tactful smile and stumbling words of condolence.

The magistrate ended the constraint with a brisk, 'Well, Miss Fletcher, this may be a bad moment to call, but the affair must be cleared up as soon as possible. The neighbourhood is in a ferment of gossip.'

'Which troubles me not at all,' I said haughtily. It was easier to deal with bluntness than with evasion.

'Oh, I'm aware the Fletchers never cared two straws for local opinion,' Mr. Fleetwood said wryly. 'I was here twenty years ago when Eben marched to Sunday service, carrying—carrying, mark you!—that slant eyed little doll he'd married. He didn't let on, but he enjoyed the sensation he caused. And when his wife vanished, and you vanished—he sent for me at the time, sent for me, mind you!—informed me that his wife was missing and he'd made other arrangements about you, and dared me to say a word to the family or to ask any more questions. I warned him folk would talk, but he said they might say what they chose. He never cared what people thought.'

'He cared only for Moonflete,' I said.

I saw Mr. Briggs glance at me with pity and my own face hardened. Pity was the one thing I did *not* want!

'The question is whether you care as little for opinion as your father did.' The magistrate brought us back firmly to the matter in hand. 'Do you propose to go on living here?'

'It's my property,' I said, and thought uneasily that I must sound like an echo of my father.

'Alone? Will you live here alone?'

I knew now what lay in his mind. Eben Fletcher had enjoyed owning people as well as places, and only Yang and Astra had failed to resent it.

I heard my own voice, calm and cool, as if I were discussing something that had nothing to do with me.

'Morally the property is not truly mine alone, nor is the income from the estate. It belongs to the village, to the mill Eben Fletcher closed down. But there is enough of my father in me to prevent my flinging everything away to charity, and not enough of him in me to make me keep my relatives dancing attendance while they wait for me to die.'

'I hear Frank Broome has gone on his travels,' Mr. Fleetwood said. 'If I were not so sorry for his poor, weak-minded mother I might have asked him a few questions about my wife's rubies.'

'Heather will probably join him as soon as she finds a buyer for Jason Hall,' I said stiffly. 'She has mentioned as much to me.'

'And Stephen and Miss Cherry?'

'Stephen is owed a considerable amount of

salary. It will enable him to set up in business on his own. Cherry will probably go to London. Miss Trimlett would be happy to chaperone her, I believe.'

Mr. Briggs nodded, but Mr. Fleetwood gave a short bark of laughter as he rose.

'You are still arranging people's lives I see, as Eben did,' he said, not unkindly but in a tone that brought colour into my face. 'No doubt you'll open up the mill too. Where will you buy your cotton?'

'From China,' Matthew said calmly from the door. He still looked pale, but he was dressed and his eyes held their usual ironic gleam. 'We will re-fit the old clipper boat and send her out to the Far East. I'd wager that the American blockade will be over in a year or two. By then we'll have the mill on its feet again.'

He had come in and taken charge as efficiently as if he were the master of the house. I felt a great surge of relief as if someone had just lifted a heavy burden from my shoulders, and my shyness of him was forgotten as I met his sudden, disarming grin.

'I shall be interested to see it.'

Mr. Fleetwood sounded doubtful as he reached for his hat.

Then we were shaking hands and Mr. Briggs was murmuring that we would meet again in the churchyard.

I waited in the garden room until Matthew returned, and knew when I looked at him again that I had not imagined the tenderness in his eyes.

'There will be a great deal of talk if you and I stay on at Moonflete, unchaperoned.'

'Not when we are wed,' he said calmly. 'And I intend to marry you soon before you begin ordering everyone around as Uncle Eben did. You may order *me* around as much as you please. I don't promise to obey, but I shall find it vastly entertaining.'

'They will say you married me for my money,' I protested weakly. 'I am not beautiful, not in the least lovable.'

'They will be fools then,' he told me. 'And you are a fool, too, saying you are not beautiful. After we are wed, I will teach you to believe the truth about yourself.'

But as he bent to embrace me, his face alight with teasing, I began to believe the truth already, and the bitterness of the past sweetened into hope for the future.

CB
JB
SL Notgood

cs.
MB VC

My Good book!

BOOKS-BY-MAIL
3301 JEFFERSON AVENUE S.W.
BIRMINGHAM, AL 35221
(205) 925-6178